The Vanished

D1500661

Books by Bill Pronzini

"Nameless Detective" Novels:

The Snatch
The Vanished
Undercurrent
Blow Back
Twospot (with Collin Wilcox)
Labyrinth
Hoodwink
Scattershot
Dragonfire
Bindlestiff
Quicksilver
Nightshades
Double (with Marcia Muller)
Bones
Deadfall
Shackles
Jackpot
Breakdown

The Vanished

Bill Pronzini

SPEAKING VOLUMES, LLC

NAPLES, FLORIDA

2011

The Vanished

ISBN 978-1-61232-063-2

One

January.

A new year, another year—but nothing really changes. The passage of Time is inexorable, but Man is a constant, Man does not change, Man loves and hates and lives and dies exactly as he did millenniums ago. The same emotions govern his actions, the same things, in essence, delight or repulse or frighten or sadden him. The chosen are still the chosen, the lonely still the lonely.

January.

The bitter-cold winter air still smells of pollution, and wars like the amusements of mad children are still being fought in alien jungles. Poverty and disease, affluence and medical science, exist side by side, and Man ignores them all in the pursuit of shelter, career, nourishment, orgasm. Nothing has changed, and nothing will, because Man is Man—and a constant.

January.

A weekday morning four days after the one night in the year which should not be spent alone, a night I had spent alone, a night when I said "Happy New Year!" to a roomful of silent emptiness and toasted Erika and toasted my convictions and toasted the fact that it was a new year and yet nothing had changed. A weekday morning like all the rest: cold, purposeless, giving birth to philosophical reflections which degenerate rapidly into little more than morbid self-pity.

1

And then the office door opens, and a ray of hope comes in, and suddenly it is not quite so dark outside or in, life is not quite so futile as it seemed seconds earlier. All you need, when you're feeling this way, is a purpose, a place to channel your energies, a way to end the maudlinism, the melancholy. All you need is your work, the thing in your life that motivates you, that brings you alive, that allows you to forget the loneliness and the emptiness of a crumbled love. That's all you need.

No. That's *part* of what you need.

But at the moment, it is enough.

Her name was Elaine Kavanaugh, and she sat stiffly, nervously, in the leather-backed chair across my desk. She was a couple of years past thirty, with short dark hair and very white skin that held an almost brittle translucence, like opaque and finely blown glass. A pair of silver-rimmed glasses gave her oval face a studious, intense appearance. When the flaps of her tailored woolen coat fell open across her joined knees, I could see the hem of a medium-length blue skirt and nicely tapering legs in dark nylon.

She was small-breasted and narrow-shouldered, but attractive enough in a fiercely virginal sort of way—the kind of girl who would cry miserably on her wedding night. And yet, there was also a strangely muted sensuality about her, a hidden-below-the-surface kind of thing, so that while you had the thought of her weeping after the consummation of marriage, you felt she would probably become an active sexual aggressor in no time at all. There were small, expensive black pearls in the lobes of her ears, and on the third finger of her left hand was a diamond-encrusted engagement ring that would have cost upward of a thousand dollars if the diamonds were genuine.

I offered her a cup of coffee, but she shook her head; I got up and refilled my own cup from the pot on the two-burner I keep and sat down again. I watched her chew diffidently at the pale iridescent lipstick on her mouth. Her eyes, behind the lens of the glasses, were a magnified coltish brown, the pupils very black, the whites clean ivory; she had them focused on a spot several inches beyond my left shoulder, and her eyelashes flicked very rapidly up and down, like miniature black hummingbirds.

She said, "I don't quite know how to begin."

"I understand," I told her. "Take your time."

"Thank you."

She cleared her throat, softly, and looked down at the large white beaded purse she was holding in her lap. While I waited for her to make up her mind to begin, I reached a cigarette out of the pack by the phone and began to roll it back and forth across the blotter without looking at it. I had been trying to give the damned things up for better than two months now, because of a fluctuating cough and a rasping in my chest that may or may not have been something worthy of medical attention; but they were the kind of habit that for some men is not easy to break, a crutch, a friend in times of stress, a thing to do with your hands and mouth and lungs when you're uptight or impatient or inactive. I had managed to cut down on my consumption from almost three packages daily to less than one, but that was the best I had been able to do; it was the best I would at any time be able to do. The cough came only in the mornings now, and I was breathing somewhat easier, more freely. I knew I should still see a doctor, but I could not seem to bring myself to do it. I had never liked doctors, not since the Second World War and the things I had seen in the field hospitals in the South Pacific.

I kept on rolling the cigarette under my index finger, resisting it, and finally Elaine Kavanaugh finished composing her thoughts and said, "I've come about my fiancé, Roy Sands. He's missing, you see."

"Missing?"

"Yes, he's disappeared."

"How do you mean, Miss Kavanaugh?"

"Well, he's just . . . vanished," she said, and made a vague, helpless gesture with her hands. "No one seems to know what happened to him." She lowered her eyes and tightened her fingers around the beaded bag. "We . . . we were to be married later this month, Roy and I, we were going to drive up to Reno and see a justice of the peace and spend our honeymoon up there . . ."

Oh Jesus, I thought, not one of these things, not now. I put the cigarette in my mouth and lit it and pulled deeply at it. As I dropped the match into the glass desk ashtray, my hand, through the exhaled smoke, seemed to look like one of those gnarled rubber affairs the kids wear on Hallowe'en.

I said, "Miss Kavanaugh . . ."

"I know what you're thinking," she said before I could get the rest of it out. "The prospective bridegroom has serious second thoughts and departs for points unknown. That's it, isn't it?"

I did not say anything.

"Well, you're wrong," she said with conviction. "I've known Roy for a long time—over two years now—and his marriage proposal wasn't one of those meaningless things made in a moment of . . . Well, we talked about it very carefully before we decided to marry, we were very sure of one another."

"I see."

"He wouldn't just run off, not this way."

"And what way is that?"

"Without telling me," she said. "Just . . . vanishing. His last letter from Germany, just a week before he came home, was very explicit about our plans. He wanted me to use part of our money for a down payment on this house I had written about in Fresno. That's where I live, you see, in Fresno."

"*Our* money, Miss Kavanaugh?"

"Yes, that's right. Roy and I have more than fifteen thousand dollars in our joint checking and savings accounts."

4

I sat up a little straighter and put my cigarette out in the ashtray; the smoke from it was like a screen between us. When the screen faded into nothingness, I said, "How much of that amount is legally your fiancé's?"

"Almost nine thousand."

"These accounts are in Fresno?"

"Yes."

"And they haven't been touched since he disappeared?"

"No, certainly not. I have the savings bankbook, and the checkbook."

I said, "Have you been to the police yet, Miss Kavanaugh?"

"Yes. They were very nice, but they said there wasn't much they could do and not to expect anything if he didn't . . . come back of his own volition."

"Uh-huh." I pulled the desk pad and pencil in front of me and wrote her name and a few other things down. "You don't have any idea where your fiancé might be?"

"No, none. I think something may have happened to Roy, an accident, amnesia . . . I don't know. I've been so worried, and this morning I just couldn't stand the waiting, the *inactivity*, and that's why I came to you. I called up my attorney and he gave me your name; he said you were very reliable."

"I hope I am, Miss Kavanaugh," I said. "Suppose you tell me something about Roy Sands?"

"Well, he's a master sergeant in the Army," she said. "I mean, he *was*. He's been in the service for twenty years, you see, and that makes him eligible for retirement with a nice pension and he chose to leave the service instead of re-enlisting when his tour came up just before Christmas. I met him at a U.S.O. dance here in San Francisco about two years ago; he was stationed at the Presidio at the time. He asked me out and then we started going together and we fell in love. After we were sure marriage was what we wanted, we made all sorts of plans and Roy bought me this ring"—she displayed the diamond engagement band with a kind of awkward pride—"and we opened the joint bank accounts just before he left for Germany."

"When was that?" I asked.

"Eleven months ago."

"Last February?"

"Yes, that's right."

"And he's been in Germany since then?"

She nodded. "Yes."

"Where?"

"At Larson Barracks, in Kitzingen."

"When did he return to the States?"

"The eighteenth of last month."

"To San Francisco for his discharge?"

"Yes. We were to spend Christmas and New Year's together."

"But you never saw him after his return, is that right?"

"Yes. I mean, no, I didn't see him."

I told myself: You weren't such a unique holiday case, guy; the world is full of lonely people. I said, "Are you sure he did return to San Francisco?"

"Oh yes," Elaine answered. "He was supposed to call me after he had arrived and gotten settled and everything, and when he didn't by Sunday night, I contacted the Presidio. They said he had come in on the flight from Germany, but no one seemed to know where he went afterward. I talked to two of Roy's friends, men who had been with him in Kitzingen and who had come over on the plane with him, and they didn't know where he'd gone either."

"What did they say about his frame of mind?"

A pair of thin horizontal lines, like furrows in a meadow of snow, appeared on her forehead. "Frame of mind?"

"Did these friends mention if he seemed happy, sad, apprehensive, nervous?"

"They said he talked about me, and about our marriage." Her voice had a slight tremor in it now. "They said I

6

shouldn't worry, everything would be all right, but I don't know. I can't help feeling . . ."

I said, "Did you write to one another regularly while he was overseas?"

She gave herself a small shake. "Yes, we were in close correspondence the entire time." She took the engagement ring between the thumb and forefinger of her right hand and rotated it from side to side, caressing it in a way that told me she was not aware of what she was doing. "I wrote to him at least twice a week, and he wrote to me three or four times a month; men aren't as ardent letter-writers as women, of course."

"He gave no indication in his letters of anything being wrong?"

"Nothing at all."

I wrote some more things on the pad. "Do you know where he's from, originally?"

"Kansas," she said. "Topeka."

"Would he still have family there?"

"Oh no, Roy is an orphan. He has no family."

"Well, what about friends or acquaintances?"

"You mean where he might be staying for some reason?"

"Yes."

"The only friends he has are in the service," she said. "I couldn't possibly know all of them, but he was stationed here in California for about three years before he was sent to Germany and he probably knew a lot of fellows who came and went."

I drank some of my coffee and looked at the package of cigarettes and looked away from it and said, "Is there anything else you can tell me that might help, Miss Kavanaugh? There's not really much here, so far."

"Well, there are the wires."

"Wires?"

"Yes, telegrams. Three days after he arrived in San Francisco—the twenty-first of December—Roy wired money to

7

three different friends who had been with him on the return flight from Germany."

"For what reason?"

"He'd lost it to them playing poker."

"How much money was involved?"

"About a hundred dollars, I think."

"He paid off everyone he'd lost to in the game?"

"Yes, there were only four of them playing."

"Where were the wires sent from?"

"Eugene, Oregon."

"Do you have any idea why your fiancé would be in Eugene?"

"No, none at all—none."

"And you didn't receive any word from Oregon yourself?"

"No, and I don't understand that at all. Why would Roy send money paying off gambling debts to his friends, but nothing whatsoever to the woman he loves, the woman he's going to marry?"

I had no answer for that. I said, "How did you find out about the wires?"

"From Chuck Hendryx. He's one of Roy's friends, the first one I talked with when I came to San Francisco. I knew him slightly from before; Roy introduced us, and we'd been over to Chuck's home in Marin County a couple of times before he and Roy left."

"Is this Hendryx still in the Army, or was he discharged too?"

"He's a full career man, with twenty-three years in now," Elaine said. "He came home for the holidays, to be with his wife and family. They don't like to travel, and so they stay here in California most of the year."

"Is he still home, do you know?"

"Yes. He'll be here until the end of January."

"Do you have his address?"

"Forty-eight Pinewood Lane, Fairfax."

"You mentioned talking to another of your fiancé's friends," I said. "Who would that be?"

"Doug Rosmond."

"Was he one of the men who got a wire from Oregon?"

She nodded. "He's home on leave also, staying with his sister Cheryl here in San Francisco. Would you want his address too?"

"Please."

She opened her bag and took out a thin address book and read me a location well out in the Parkside District, on Vicente near Ocean Beach. I wrote it down on the pad.

"You said money was wired to three friends, Miss Kavanaugh. Can you tell me the name of the third?"

"A man named Gilmartin, I think."

"Gil Martin?"

"No, Gilmartin—one word. I can't recall his first name."

"You didn't talk with him, then?"

"No, but Chuck did. He didn't know anything that would help, either."

I rubbed the pencil eraser across the bridge of my nose. "Did you check with the authorities in Eugene?"

"No. The Missing Persons people here told me they would do that."

"They apparently learned nothing, or you would have been notified by now."

"Yes," she said in a small voice.

"Is there anything further you can tell me, anything at all?"

"I've thought and thought, and there's just nothing." She met my eyes directly now, and hers seemed huge and imploring behind her glasses. "You do believe me that Roy hasn't just . . . run off somewhere, don't you? I mean, you agree that the circumstances are very strange surrounding his disappearance?"

"They would seem to be, yes," I said carefully.

"Then you'll investigate for me?"

"As long as you understand that the odds of one man locating another, when the law enforcement agencies haven't been able to do it, are not the best in the world."

She nodded positively. "I understand—but there *is* the chance, and that's all that matters now."

"If I do locate him, my liability terminates with that location. I would simply tell you where he is, and after that it's up to you."

She caressed her ring in that secret way again. "Yes, that's fine," she said softly.

I told her what I charged, plus expenses, and she said that was perfectly acceptable. I got one of the standard business contract forms from my desk and filled it in and had her sign it; then I gave her a copy and she gave me a check for one hundred dollars as a retainer.

I said, "Will you authorize my going up to Oregon? It would seem necessary, and I'll have to fly."

"Yes, certainly."

"Do you have a picture of your fiancé, by any chance?"

"I gave the only good one I had to the Missing Persons—but I do have a sketch of him."

"Sketch?"

"Yes, he must have had it done by one of those sidewalk artists in Europe somewhere. He had all his belongings sent to me in Fresno just before he came home. Naturally, I didn't look through them right away, I don't believe in prying—but when he disappeared as he did, I . . . well, I went over everything very carefully. There was no clue to where he might have gone, but I did find the sketch. I think he must have intended to surprise me with it later on."

"Did you happen to bring it with you?"

Elaine moved her head affirmatively. "I knew you'd need a picture," she said. She took from her coat pocket a rolled sheet of that type of heavy rag paper which comes as part of an artist's sketch pad. She handed it across to me. I took it and slipped off a blue rubber band and unrolled the paper, smoothing it out flat on my desk.

It was fourteen-by-eighteen in size, a head-and-shoulders sketch without background, done in pastel chalk over which a lacquer-type fixative had been applied. I know very little about art, but it seemed to me that the artist who had drawn the portrait was gifted with real talent; it was faintly expressionistic, with bold lines and heavy shadows and somewhat enlarged features, rather than an example of classic portraiture. The man it depicted was about my own age, middle-to-late forties; he had dark-brown hair with a little wave in it and gray eyes and the kind of nose that is often described as aquiline. His mouth was curved in a faint, boyish grin, and he possessed a kind of rugged, craggy, masculine virility.

I looked up at Elaine. "How good a likeness is this?"

"Really quite good," she answered. Her eyes shone, and I knew Roy Sands was in her mind, vivid and smiling just for her. "It captures the . . . oh, I don't know, the *essence* of Roy. I don't know how else to put it."

I looked at the sketch a little more, and then rolled it up again and slid the rubber band around it. I set it to one side of my blotter. "All right, Miss Kavanaugh," I said gently. "Could you tell me where you're staying?"

"The Royal Gate Hotel, on Powell Street."

I made a note of that, and then we got on our feet and touched hands and said some things to one another—mild entreaties and milder reassurances. I showed her to the door and watched her walk down the hall to the elevator. She walked very stiffly, her head pulled back, resignation in her step, and it was like watching a prisoner walking a cell-block, a prisoner with nothing waiting for her except a barred cell and an endless succession of solitary nights and hopelessly shattered dreams.

It was a painful image, fraught with symbolic meaning. I shook myself a little and closed the door and went back to my desk for a cigarette.

Two

Pinewood Lane was a narrow blacktopped road that wound and curled and doubled back on itself through the thickly wooded foothills behind Fairfax—a half-hour drive north across the Golden Gate Bridge. The homes were spaced well apart, and you had occasional glimpses of shingled alpine roofs or railed verandas or huge rectangles of glass hidden among the towering conifers and eucalyptus. It took some money, and a taste for nature and the sequestered life, to live up there; I wondered if those who had them knew how potentially blessed they were in a time of increasing universal hunger, overpopulation, and ecological apathy.

I found number forty-eight without difficulty. There was a gateless stone arch at the foot of the entrance drive, with the numerals 48 carved out of pinewood at the center of the curvature. I drove beneath that and followed the drive through thick, velvety green firs, climbing slightly and somewhat circuitously.

I glanced down at the temperature gauge as I drove, and it registered hot, as it had begun to do several miles back. The car had not run properly since it had been severely damaged during the course of a kidnapping case I had been involved in a couple of months previously—a sordid and lamentable business because it had directly precipitated the split between Erika and me, and for several other reasons as well. I had had the car in to the garage three times in the past six weeks, and it looked as if I would have to take it in again, with the engine overheating the way it was.

The drive came out of the evergreens finally and hooked sharply to the left, ending in a small clearing at the rear of which sat a large, rustic home raised off the earth on heavy wood pillars. It was constructed of bleached-pine board-ing, with a wide veranda running the width of it and ex-tending back on both sides. The wall of the house was solid glass, except for a wooden area beneath the roof peak. On my right, a steep set of stairs rose up to the veranda and what I assumed would be the main entrance.

I parked near the stairs and got out of the car into a whistling, ice-tinged wind; it was as cold over here as it had been in San Francisco, in spite of a pale winter sun setting up a shimmering glare overhead. I started up the stairs, and a door opened above and a man came out onto the veranda carrying a tumbler filled with ice and a liquid that appeared by its color to be either Scotch or bourbon. Like Sands, he was about my age, and he wore slacks and a hand-tooled leather vest open over a white turtleneck. He was about my size and height, too, starting to paunch in the same way I had but consciously sucking in on it in a kind of grimly determined struggle to maintain a youthful physique.

I reached the top of the stairs and he said, "Hi, I'm Chuck Hendryx. You must be the guy who called."

I said that I was. Before driving all the way up here, I had gotten him on the phone and told him my name and why I wanted to see him, and he had said he would be home all day and to drop by at my convenience. I had intended to talk to Doug Rosmond first, since he was considerably closer, but there had been no answer when I tried his sister's num-ber. I had also telephoned the Missing Persons Bureau at the Hall of Justice before leaving my office; they had nothing for me on the disappearance of Roy Sands.

Hendryx and I shook hands and sized one another up the way two men will do, meeting for the first time. He was thick-shouldered, with a wedge-shaped face and bright, alert brown eyes set deeply above his wide cheekbones. He was losing his hair—a dark sandy color—and making a desperate attempt to conceal it by intricate machinations with a comb; when it really started to go, in another couple of years, I had the thought that he would probably buy one of those permanent toupees that you can wear underwater or while sky-diving out of airplanes. There were two small moles on either side of his large mouth, like two boulders marking the entrance to a cave; but the smile which quirked his lips assured you that there was nothing ominous or unfriendly lurking within.

Hendryx apparently decided I was all right. He said, "Come on inside, it's colder than the proverbial witch's tit out here. My wife and kids are home, but they won't bother us."

We went through the door and into a beam-ceilinged living room done in light hues that complemented the bleached-pine walls. The floor was parqueted pine, bare except for a couple of circular braided rugs. The far wall was fashioned of buff-colored brick, and a three-foot square opening cut off-center served as a fireplace; there were several logs burning in there—green pitch pine that hissed and crackled and sent up rainbow sparks in a miniature fireworks display. The place was clean and neat enough, but it held a vague air of stiffness, as if its natural state were one of perpetual chaos.

Hendryx shut the door and gestured toward one of the upholstered chairs. "Sit down, make yourself comfortable. Drink?"

"Thanks, no."

He looked a little ruefully at the tumbler in his hand. "Too damned early for it, really, but I need something to bolster my courage. You got any kids?"

"No," I said. "I'm not married."

"Christ, I wish I wasn't sometimes. Not that I don't love

15

my old lady, or the three boys, but you live away from 'em most of the year and you can't get used to 'em again. It's like being in a kind of limbo: half-bachelor, half-married, you know?"

"Well," I said, and shrugged.

"Sure," Hendryx said. "That kind of life does have its advantages, though." He gave me a broad wink.

I smiled, because it was the only thing for me to do, and thought: The old double standard. Well, he looks like the sybaritic type, all right—Don Juan at the crossroads. I wonder if his family doesn't like traveling because he doesn't want them to like traveling? Oh, the hell with that; you're becoming a righteous fart in your old age.

I watched Hendryx sit down on the divan across from me and put his tumbler on the heavy glass top of a wrought-iron coffee table. He got a cigarette from a pocket in his vest and lighted it and threw the match on the floor without any compunction at all. And I thought now: The world is full of slobs, too. Brother, meet a brother. But this place could never hold a candle to my apartment, even in its natural state.

I said, "As I told you on the phone, Mr. Hendryx, I've been asked to investigate the disappearance of Roy Sands."

"By Elaine Kavanaugh, uh-huh. Well, I don't blame her for calling a guy like you into it; the cops haven't given her any satisfaction, and she's shook up and has the right to be. It's a damned peculiar thing, Roy vanishing like that."

"You don't think he may have changed his mind about marrying the girl? Or had second thoughts, anyway, and went off somewhere to think it over?"

"Hell no," Hendryx said emphatically. "He wanted to marry her, all right. He was kind of a close-mouthed guy, but when he did talk personal things, it was mostly this Elaine. He'd fallen for her, no doubt about that, and marriage was what he wanted."

16

"Then he felt strongly toward her when he came back to the States last month?"

"Sure. He mentioned her name a couple of times on the plane, and you could see it in his eyes. He asked me and Doug Rosmond and Rich Gilmartin if we'd come to the wedding—sometime this month, I think he said. He had one of us picked out as best man, but he wouldn't say who. We all agreed to go; hell, he's a buddy and we're kind of a team, you know? He was supposed to contact us after Christmas sometime and let us know the arrangements."

"Did you talk with Sands after your arrival in San Francisco?"

"For a couple of minutes the day after—Sunday," Hendryx answered. "He'd gone through processing, and he was on his way out of the Presidio wearing civvies and carrying a small suitcase."

"Did he mention where he was going?"

"Well, I kidded him about Elaine, you know, but he was in this sober mood—the way he'd get sometimes when a thing was on his mind. He said he was planning to see her pretty soon, but that he had something to take care of first, up north."

"Up north?"

"That's what he said."

"Just that, no specific place?"

"Nope."

"And he didn't elaborate on the business he had to take care of?"

Hendryx shook his head. "At the time I figured if he wanted to tell me about it, he would have."

"Do you have any idea what it was?"

"Not a one."

"Did he have any friends that you know about in the Pacific Northwest? Oregon, for example?"

"The only friends Roy had were his service buddies," Hendryx said. "I told him more than once that he ought to re-up, marry Elaine and bring her with him, but she wanted a house and kids, that kind of crap, and she'd talked him into it too. He would be lost at first, you know? He doesn't make friends that easy."

"He say anything to you before he left the Presidio?"

"The usual: so long, keep it limp—like that."

"That was the last time you talked to him, then?"

"Yeah."

I started to ask him about the wires from Oregon, but before I could, there was the sound of a car coming into the clearing out front. A horn blared several times, shrilly, and Hendryx got to his feet. "Company," he said. "Hang on, will you?"

"Sure."

He went to the door and through it. I sat watching the dying curls of smoke from his cigarette, moistening my lips a little and rubbing the palms of my hands across my trouser legs. I had had seven cigarettes already today, and if I wanted to keep my consumption under a pack every twenty-four hours I was going to have to start rationing.

To have something to do with my hands, I took the rolled sketch of Roy Sands from my inside jacket pocket; I had put it there, along with the notes I had taken during the interview with Elaine Kavanaugh, just prior to leaving the office. I unrolled the sketch and looked again at Sands' likable face and wondered what sort of trouble he could have gotten himself into. People don't disappear without good cause; and if a change of heart about marriage had not prompted Sands into momentary hermitage—and I was inclined to believe Elaine that it hadn't—then the set of circumstances she had outlined meant that he was very definitely in some kind of tight.

The sound of male voices on the veranda preceded the opening of the door by a couple of seconds, and then Hendryx came back inside. With him was a second man a couple of years younger. This guy was lean and wiry and eight inches under six feet, and you knew immediately that he had taken a lot of abuse concerning his height over the years, and that he would be constantly on the defensive about it. He owned a wealth of graying-brown hair, worn long and shaggy and combed into drifts on a narrow skull to give him added stature; in addition, he sported a thick, silky-looking mustache—one of these fashionable Continental jobs that slant down to the chin on both sides of the mouth—and there was some gray in that too. Intelligent brown eyes peered out from under question-mark brows, and he carried himself with an air of confident, no-bullshit masculinity; he would do a lot of talking, and command a lot of attention, and be hell-on-wheels in a back-to-back barroom brawl.

Hendryx led the guy over to where I was, and I got on my feet for the introductions. The bantamweight was Rich Gilmartin, which made things a little easier for me since I had planned on looking up Sands' third Army buddy later on; he had just dropped by, he said, for a quick one and to see if Chucko wanted to sit in on a stud game some cats were setting up in San Rafael tomorrow night. Hendryx explained who I was and why I was there, and then went to a portable bar against the side wall to fix drinks.

Gilmartin started away toward one of the chairs, hesitated, and turned back to me. He looked down at the partially unrolled sketch in my left hand—I hadn't had time to put it away—and said, "Isn't that Roy?"

I admitted that it was.

"You mind?"

"No, go ahead."

He took the sketch and held it up and looked at it, cocking his head to one side. "Damn fine likeness," he said at length. "Where'd you get it?"

"From his fiancée."

"He send it to her from Germany?"

"In a way," I said. "It was among the things he forwarded

to Fresno. She didn't have an extra photo, and this serves the purpose just as well."

"Who would have figured old Roy for an artist's model?" Gilmartin said. He took the sketch over to Hendryx. "What do you think, Chucko?"

"Pretty good, all right."

"Damn fine likeness," Gilmartin said again. He took the drink Hendryx gave him and came back and returned the sketch to me. "So you've joined the hunt for Roy."

"That's right."

"I hope to Christ you can do more than the cops have been able to. He's just another name on the Missing Persons blotter as far as they're concerned."

"I'll do what I can."

"Sure, that's all anybody can expect."

"Do you have any idea where Sands could be, Mr. Gilmartin?"

"Rich—that's why we got Christian names, right? No, I don't know where Roy could be. I've kicked this disappearance around with Dougie and Chucko, but it just doesn't make any sense. No sense at all."

Hendryx brought over a fresh drink for himself. "Sure you won't have one?" he asked me.

"A little early, thanks."

"It's never a little early for good Scotch," Gilmartin said. He drank deeply from his glass. "I needed this, Chucko. Hell of a night last night."

"Yeah?"

"You remember that redhead works at the Mill?"

"Don't tell me you finally scored with that?"

"Oh baby! And she was just like I said she'd be: a French postcard. A real French postcard, Chucko."

"No lie, huh?"

"Oh baby!"

The three of us sat down. I rolled up the sketch of Roy Sands and put it away inside my jacket, and then listened to

Gilmartin explain in detail what had taken place with the redhead the night before. Hendryx absorbed every word in rapt attention. From somewhere at the rear of the house, I could hear the faint rumble of an automatic dryer and the half-muffled voice of a woman reprimanding a child; I shifted uncomfortably in my chair.

I said, "Do you mind if we talk about Roy Sands?"

They both looked at me, and Hendryx said, "Well, sure, go ahead."

"What can you tell me about these wires from Oregon?"

"Not much. He sent them to me and Doug and Rich a couple of days before Christmas."

"It was to pay off some money he'd lost in a poker game, is that right?"

"Right," Gilmartin said. "We'd played a little stud the night before we left Larson, and he had lousy cards all night. He was a little strapped then, Christmas and mustering out, the whole bag, and so he wrote out some IOU's and said he'd get the money to us as soon as he could."

"Did it seem odd that he would pay off minor gambling debts by wire?"

"Why should it? Roy likes to keep his debts current. We used to play stud and gin rummy, a bunch of us, a couple-three times a week over there, and if Roy lost and couldn't settle then and there, he'd always have the money first thing on payday."

"Well, he could have paid all of you when he saw you before his wedding, couldn't he?"

"Yeah, right, but like I told you, Roy is funny that way. He likes everything even up, him into nobody and nobody into him."

I looked at Hendryx. "Did he mention the debts when you saw him at the Presidio?"

"Not that I remember."

"If he'd had the money then, he'd have paid you, wouldn't he?"

"Sure, if he'd had it."

"He had it two days later," I said.

Hendryx frowned. "Say, that's right."

"Would he have gotten his mustering-out pay by that time?"

"No chance," Gilmartin said. "Besides, he was having everything sent to his chick in Fresno."

I thought that over a little. "He didn't get any money from her," I said, "and he didn't go near his savings or checking account. But he had to have gotten the money he paid you with from somewhere."

"Yeah, he did."

"Would you know if he had a private account here in the States, something he might not have told Elaine Kavanaugh about?"

"Not old Roy. Hell, I know for a fact most of his pay went to her for banking. He was really hooked, poor bastard."

I shifted position on the chair to get rid of a cramp forming in my left hip. "Was there a message along with the money Sands wired you?"

"Just a few words on mine."

"Did you happen to save it?"

"No reason to at the time."

"What about you?" I asked Hendryx.

"Same thing. Mine went into the fireplace."

"Can either of you remember what was said?"

"Here's the thirty I owe you and have a Merry Christmas—something like that."

"Ditto," Gilmartin said.

I nodded, and did some more thinking. At length I said, "Is there anything at all you can think of that might help me locate Sands? Something in his past, something he may have let slip at one time or another?"

Hendryx frowned and ran a hand carefully over the thinning hair on the crown of his head. He said, "No, nothing." Gilmartin rolled the sweating surface of his glass over his

22

forehead; with his other hand he made a negative gesture.

I could not think of anything else I wanted to ask either of them, and so I said, "I guess that's it," and got on my feet. I thanked them for their time, shook hands with them, promised to let them know if I learned anything definite. Hendryx said I could call on Rich and him any time if there was anything further they could do, and then I went out and down the steps to my car.

I sat there for a moment, listening to the wind sing a sad, humming song through the high green trees. I wondered, oddly, if the topic of conversation behind the glass up there was Roy Sands or a redheaded French postcard; then I got the thing going and went away without looking back.

Three

As I slowed to pay the southbound toll on the Golden Gate Bridge, I thought it might be an idea to drive over to Vicente Street—not far from there—and see if Doug Rosmond had come home. I did not much feel like going back to the dusty emptiness of my office, and the car was running all right since I had stopped to put water in the radiator after leaving Pinewood Lane.

I took the 19th Avenue exit off the toll plaza and drove through Golden Gate Park and turned westward on Vicente. There was no fog today—not yet anyway—and from the vicinity of Cheryl Rosmond's home you could see the slate-gray water of the Pacific beyond Ocean Beach. It had the kind of desolate appearance the sea achieves in winter, primitive and unsettling, like looking at something out of the dim past. Like the deserts and the majestic mountain ranges, the oceans were something else that did not change with the passage of time.

The number Elaine Kavanaugh had given me was a white box-shaped rough-stucco house identical to its neighbors on both sides of the street, crowded together in long rows like beads on a tightly strung necklace. It had a small square of lawn, and a wide set of wooden stairs inside a stucco frame leading up to the front entrance. White filmy curtains covered the rectangular window to one side.

I parked my car at the curb and got out and climbed the

steps. The wind blowing in from the sea was harsh and pene-trating, and I hunched my neck in the collar of my topcoat as I pressed the doorbell. I stood waiting, shivering a little, but no one opened the door. I put my thumb against the bell and rang it again, and then there were faint sounds within, someone approaching. I was in luck after all. A night bolt scraped inside and the door parted inward.

The first thing—the only thing—I saw were her eyes.

They were huge and very green and very soft, expressive and warm and yet containing a kind of pleading, like a child after a severe punishment saying *no more, no more.* And there was sensitivity, too, in their depths, and tragedy and gaiety and sensuality, and I thought with a small part of my mind: What's the matter with you, you can't be seeing all of those things, and yet I *was* seeing them, they were all there for me to see and interpret.

There was something in my eyes for her, too. I became aware of that very suddenly, and I wondered dimly if she was reading the same things I was, if a similar kind of inner reflection was there for her as well.

Neither of us moved for several long seconds; then, finally, she made a soft meaningless sound deep in her throat and put her hand up at the edge of the door, as if she were thinking of shutting it. I tried to find something to say to her, but I could not seem to think of anything. I looked at the rest of her, and I was in no way disappointed: small, slender hands; long flowing hair the soft reddish-gold of autumn leaves; no makeup, but none needed to accentuate elfin fea-tures as symmetrical as expert sculpturing. She could have been twenty-seven or thirty-two—a totally unimportant fac-tor—and she was soft and gently rounded in a pale lavender skirt and a white sweater with lavender bands like narrow epaulets across the shoulders.

"What is it?" she said then, in a voice that was just a shade too high.

I felt awkward suddenly, and my hands seemed large

and curiously spasmodic. I got them down into the pockets of my overcoat. "Is . . . Are you Cheryl Rosmond?"

"Yes? What is it you want?"

"I'd like to talk to your brother. Doug Rosmond?"

"Oh," she said, and her hand dropped away from the door. There seemed to be a faint flush just under her small ears.

"Is he at home, Miss Rosmond?"

"Yes, he's here."

I told her my name and my profession. I couldn't take my eyes off her face, but she was not looking at me at all now; her gaze was to the left of me and beyond, counting the cracks in the sidewalk, the blades of grass in the lawn. "I've been hired to locate a man named Roy Sands, a friend of your brother's; he's disappeared."

"I know," she said. "I don't understand it."

"Do you know Sands?"

"Yes. We . . . Yes."

"May I come in, Miss Rosmond?"

"Of course. Doug is on the back porch, fixing the drain on the laundry sink. I'll get him."

"Thank you."

She backed away, and I entered and shut the door. It was pleasant in there, warmly comfortable: curving mahogany sectional and matching chairs upholstered in pink and pastel-yellow, white alabaster lamps giving off warm light through shantung shades, staggered knickknack shelves on one wall with glass and porcelain figurines of owls and elephants and horses. The floor was almost completely covered by a muted-patterned rug.

Cheryl kept on backing away, looking at me, and then away, and then back. She said, "I'll get Doug," and turned abruptly through a doorway.

When I was alone, I took my hands out of my pockets and stared at them. They looked faintly gray, the veins bluish and prominent. I put them away again and went around the room, looking at the pictures on the walls without really seeing them.

A voice said my name, and when I turned, a guy in the same age bracket as Hendryx and Gilmartin was standing in the doorway through which Cheryl had gone moments earlier. She was not with him. I wondered if she had gone to some other part of the house, where she could not hear her brother and me—or whether she was out there in the kitchen, at the stove or at the drainboard, listening and maybe thinking about me in the same way I was thinking about her . . .

I shook myself mentally and got my mind focused on Doug Rosmond. He was coming toward me now, a big, quiet-looking man dressed in a gray sweatshirt and old, dusty jeans. He was her brother, all right: the same reddish-gold hair, his thick and unkempt; the same green eyes; the same symmetrical features—though in his case distinctly masculine. He would have had a lot of women in his time, I thought—he was the kind of guy they felt instinctively protective toward, the maternal instinct—but unlike men such as Hendryx and Gilmartin, he would have left each of them with their pride and their self-respect afterward; there was no hint of cruelty or cynical contempt in his face or his steady gaze.

We got the amenities over with, and I sat on one of the chairs. He went over to lean against an inexpensive television-and-stereo unit nearby; I supposed it was because he did not want to sit on the furniture with his dusty clothing.

"I'm glad to hear that Elaine Kavanaugh called a detective in to help find Roy," he said. "She was pretty worried about him when I talked to her."

"When was that, Mr. Rosmond?"

"A couple of days ago, the last time. She called to find out if I'd heard anything from Roy. Just grabbing at straws, I guess."

"Do you have any ideas where Sands might be?"

"No—none, I'm afraid."

"I take it you don't think he went off of his own accord?"

"Not the way he felt about Elaine, not without telling her he was going," Rosmond said. "Besides that, Roy isn't the kind of guy to just disappear unexpectedly—like a boozer will, sometimes, or an outdoors type, or a guy with a lot of independence."

The booze angle had occurred to me briefly on the drive back from Marin County. I said, "Sands isn't much of a drinker?"

"Not Roy. Puke and pass out on three shots and sick for two days afterward—that kind of guy. A couple of beers nursed out over an evening is his limit."

So much for that possibility. I asked Rosmond some of the same questions I had asked Hendryx and Gilmartin earlier, and got the same general answers: Sands was basically introverted, a gambler and hell-raiser only in the mildest sense, and an all-around nice guy. There was nothing in any of that, or if there was, I couldn't see it; I was having a difficult time keeping my mind orderly because of Cheryl, and I found my eyes straying toward the open doorway to the kitchen from time to time.

I lit a cigarette and told Rosmond about Hendryx's meeting with Sands at the Presidio. I asked, "Did Sands ever mention business or acquaintances, anything at all, in the Pacific Northwest?"

"Not that I know of. Well, wait, there's a guy named Jackson, Nick Jackson, I think, that came from Oregon or Washington originally. Roy had some trouble with him a while back, at the Presidio."

"What sort of trouble?"

"Well"—he lowered his voice—"Roy was sleeping with Jackson's woman and Jackson didn't like it; this was maybe three years back, before he met Elaine. Jackson was a major then, and he tried to railroad Roy into a dishonorable, and maybe some time in the stockade, because of it."

29

"How so?"

"There was a little black-marketeering going on—cigarettes, booze, stuff like that. Roy didn't have a damned thing to do with it, but Jackson tried to make out that he did."

"What happened?"

"Nothing. They caught the guys who were doing it."

"No repercussions between Sands and Jackson?"

"Bad feelings, maybe, but nothing rough."

"Anything since?"

"Not that I know about."

"Do you have any idea where Jackson is now?"

"No. He's not at the Presidio, though."

"I'll check on it."

"I doubt if Jackson could have had anything to do with Roy's disappearance. I mean, the trouble *was* three years ago."

"You never know," I said. I worked on my cigarette a little. "There's no reason you're aware of for Sands having gone to Oregon from San Francisco?"

"I can't think of any."

"This money he wired you just before Christmas, to pay off his poker losses—do you happen to have the message that came with it?"

"As a matter of fact, I do," Rosmond said. "I'm one of these guys who never likes to throw anything out, and after it came I put it with some papers in one of my bags."

"Would you mind if I had a look at it?"

"Not at all. I'll get it for you."

He left the room and there was the sound of a door opening, and closing, and then there was only silence. I sat smoking, listening to the quiet, and I had this foolish impulse to go out into the kitchen to see if Cheryl was there. I got up and took a couple of steps and stopped and thought: What the hell are you doing? Christ! I sat down again.

I could not get her out of my mind. It happens that way sometimes, and there's no explanation for it, no rationality involved. You meet a woman, however briefly, and you can't stop thinking about her, touching her with your mind, examining some distinctive feature over and over again. With Cheryl it was her eyes, it would always be her eyes; I could see them once more, mentally, and all the things they had contained, and the reflection in them of what she had in turn discovered in my own eyes . . .

I heard the opening and closing of a door again, reverse process. Rosmond came back into the room with a folded square of paper in his right hand.

"Here it is," he said, and gave me the paper and went over by the television-and-stereo unit again. I unfolded the square and spread it open on my knee. It read:

eunmx xlt 1960 js nl pd eugene ore 12/21 830p

douglas rosmond
2579 vicente st san francisco/calif

here is the 27 i owe you buddy. merry christmas roy

It told me nothing that I was not already aware of, except that the wires had been sent around 8:30 P.M. on the twenty-first of last month. I handed the telegram back to Rosmond.

He said, "Not much help, is it?"

"No," I said, "not much."

"Roy was forever doing crazy things like that. I had three weeks leave in Italy once, and he sent me twenty bucks in cash that he'd borrowed from me, instead of waiting till I got back to Germany." Rosmond worried a hand through his hair. "I wish I could give you something that *would* help, but I just can't. Roy never talked much about his personal life—except for Elaine Kavanaugh. He didn't have much choice there, since we all knew about him dating her and planning to marry her when his twenty was up."

"I don't suppose there's a chance that he could have been

dangling another woman here in the States," I said. "That might explain his trip to Oregon."

"No chance at all," Rosmond said positively. "Roy used to cat around as much as the rest of us until he met Elaine, but he was a changed guy after she came on the scene. When he fell, he fell hard."

"Is there anybody else in this area who might know something about Sands' disappearance or whereabouts? Another close friend of his? An acquaintance?"

"Just Rich and Chuck and me. Nobody else—except maybe Jock MacVeagh, but he's still at Larson. The five of us used to buddy around regularly over there."

"Well, I guess that's it, then."

"Are you planning to go up to Oregon to look for Roy?"

"I guess I will. I haven't learned anything that might help down here, and Eugene is the next logical step."

Rosmond rumpled his hair again. "I'd hate to . . . Oh, the hell with that kind of thinking. Roy can take care of himself." He came away from the console unit. "Luck, huh?"

"Thanks," I said.

I got on my feet and we shook hands and there was nothing I could do then but cross the room to the door with him. I wanted to say something about Cheryl, but what could I say? I wanted to see her again, if only for a moment, before I left—but I could figure no plausible way to work that. All that was left was for me to open the door and exchange good-byes with Rosmond, and then I was outside in the cold wind coming off the ocean, walking down to my car, stopping and turning and looking up at the house for a moment.

I thought I saw movement at the window, behind the curtains, a flash of trailing reddish-gold, a flash of lavender-and-white, but it may have been only my imagination.

32

Four

When I got back to my office on Taylor Street, a couple of blocks up from Market, it was a quarter past three. I put the morning coffee on to reheat, and while I waited for it to come to a boil, I rang up my answering service to find out if anyone had called during my absence. No one had.

I stood back and looked the place over with a critical eye: the old oak desk and a couple of chairs, like a general and two enlisted men of a badly defeated army, weary and battle-scarred; outside the rail divider a dusty couch and a table with some back-date magazines that had never been opened by me or by anyone else; a narrow alcove with a sink and some shelves for stationery supplies—bathroom facilities down the hall, turn to your right, but somehow the janitor never remembers to refill the paper dispenser so you had better bring something of your own; and a single metal file cabinet with the hot plate and the coffee pot resting on top of it and nothing much inside. It was always cold in there, even with the valve on the steam radiator opened wide, and the air was always a little musty, a little stale. Some place, I thought. Some occupant, too.

Knock it off, I thought.

I rescued the coffee and carried a mug of it back to the desk and sat down and stared out the window for a time. There was nothing much to see except the stone-and-glass buildings outlined against a cold gray winter sky. It seemed

33

that every time I looked, another skyscraper was going up, taller and taller, like mushrooms or toadstools sprouting with that alarming rapidity after a heavy rain—the fungi of the cities . . .

Well, nuts to that too. Come down again, for Christ's sake. Did she get to you that much?

Yeah, I thought, she got to me that much.

All right then.

I pulled the phone in front of me and took the note pad from my suit jacket. I dialed the number I had looked up earlier, and it rang once, twice, and the palm of my hand was faintly moist around the receiver. Another ring, and a soft click, and she said, "Hello?"

"Miss Rosmond?"

I heard the intake of her breath, and then I listened to silence and the hammering of the radiator. Pretty soon she said, "Yes, who is this?" even though I was certain she already knew.

I said my name for her, just to make it absolute. Then: "I was wondering if I could see you tonight? I thought, since you know Roy Sands personally, you might be able to tell me something that would help my investigation—"

"I don't know anything that would help. What could I possibly know that my brother doesn't?"

"I just thought—"

"I'm sorry."

I had the feeling that she was about to hang up. I said quickly, "I'd like to see you tonight anyway. For dinner and a show, or just for a drink. Whatever you say."

Ten seconds crawled away. And she said, "I . . . don't think so."

"Why not?"

"I just . . . don't think so."

"Miss Rosmond—Cheryl—I'd like to see you."

No response.

"I could meet you for a drink," I said. "Just for an hour or so. Anywhere you like."

34

I did some more waiting, and the palms of my hands were still moist. She said finally, in a low voice, "I suppose . . . I guess we could have a drink."

"Shall I meet you somewhere?"

"Do you know the Golden Door, on Irving off Nineteenth?"

"Yes, I know it."

"I'll be there at nine."

"At nine, Cheryl."

"Good-bye," she said, and she was gone.

I put the receiver down, thinking: She's been hurt in some way, badly hurt, and that's why she's got this defensive barrier up, why she's so hesitant. But she's lonely, too, even lonelier than I am, and she's willing to take the chance, willing to find out if there's anything to this attraction we both felt.

I began to feel considerably better. This meeting tonight could be the beginning of something good for both of us, given enough time and patience and understanding. Something very good.

An end to loneliness.

They were digging up the pavement a half-block from my apartment in Pacific Heights, and I had to park four streets away and walk back. The staccato chattering of jackhammers and the diesel roar of trucks were deafening. As if parking in Pacific Heights wasn't impossible enough, the goddamn city.

I turned into the foyer of my building, a tired old Victorian lady clinging to the time-tattered remnants of elegance, looking backward to the era when she had been a fine private home and no one had anticipated a global war. She still commanded a high price because of her location, and I could not have afforded her if it were not for the fact that I had lived with her for almost eighteen years under the singular supervision of a benevolent landlord.

There was no mail in my box, and no respite from the

noise inside my second-floor flat; even with all the windows closed and locked, you could hear the volume of sound in the street outside. I went through the cluttered living room, stepping over this and kicking that aside. I was at an age, and had a temperament, that no longer required care and neatness. As I had suspected Hendryx of being, I was a slob —not proud of it, just accepting it.

I got a beer out of the refrigerator, re-entered the living room, and sat down on the couch. From there I could see the laminated-wood shelving which covered the side wall beyond the bay windows, and which contained better than five thousand copies of detective and adventure pulp magazines I had collected over the years. That was my one hobby, the accumulation of pulps, and when I was feeling low I could usually immerse myself in an issue of *Black Mask* or *Dime Detective*, or one of the other seventy-five titles I possessed, thoroughly enough to circumvent the mood.

The lurid covers, some of which I had placed so that they faced into the room, made a nice contrast to the heavy, ponderous pseudo-Hepplewhite furniture, the faded rose-design rug and wallpaper. The magazines were segregated by title and date, and I had an index made up so that when I received a quote from one of the suppliers I dealt with, I could easily check what I had against the for-sale listing.

I sipped some of my beer, and Cheryl was on my mind, and the missing Roy Sands—and Erika, too, as she always seemed to be when I was conscious of my pulp magazines. Every time I looked at them, I could hear the words Erika had said to me in this very room some two and a half months ago, harsh and stinging words: *"You want to know the real reason you quit the police force to open up that agency of yours, the real deep-down reason? I'll tell you: it's an obsession to be just like those pulp-magazine detectives and you never would have been satisfied until you'd tried it. Well, now you've tried it, for ten years you've tried it, and you just don't want to let go, you can't let go. You're living in a world that doesn't exist and never did, in an era that's twenty-five-years dead. You're a kid dreaming about being a hero, and yet you haven't got the guts or the flair to go out and be one; you're too honest and too sensitive and too ethical, too affected by real corruption and real human misery to be the kind of lone wolf private eye you'd like to be. You're no damned hero, and it hurts you that you're not, and that's why you won't let go of it. And the whole while you're eating and sleeping and living yesteryear's dream world, to salve your wounded pride you're deluding yourself that you're an anachronism in a real-life world that couldn't care less one way or the other. You're nothing but a little boy, and I'm damned if I'll have a little boy in my bed every night of the year . . ."*

The thing of it was, the thing I could never make her understand, was that even if she was right, it did not matter—it was not important. How I became what I am, or why, is irrelevant to the simple fact that I am what I am. I could not change, for her or for anyone. But that had not been enough for Erika, and it had ended between us for primarily that reason.

And now, maybe, after two and a half empty months, there was Cheryl.

I finished my beer and went into the cluttered bedroom and dragged my battered suitcase out of the closet. I had called United Airlines from my office and made a reservation on the 9:00 A.M. flight to Eugene the following morning; as I had told Doug Rosmond, that was my next logical step on behalf of Elaine Kavanaugh. I had also called Elaine at her hotel to ask about this Jackson, the one Rosmond had mentioned as once having had trouble with Roy Sands. She did not know who Jackson was, and could not recall Sands' ever using the name in any context whatsoever. I had also rung up Chuck Hendryx, and that call had netted me a little more information.

Hendryx had said, "Sure, I remember the trouble Roy had with that prick Jackson. I didn't know he was from the

Northwest, though, and that's why I didn't say anything about it."

"Do you know where Jackson is now?"

"Well, the last I heard he was on Okie."

"Okinawa?"

"Yeah."

"When was that?"

"Last year sometime. One of the boys at Larson happened to mention his name."

My final call before leaving the office had been to a guy named Salzberg, who was an Army lieutenant stationed at the Presidio and whom I had known for thirty years, since the Second War. We had talked a little, and then I had asked him if he'd bend regulations a bit and find out about this Nick Jackson for me; since Jackson had been stationed at the Presidio three years ago, there would be a file on him that would have a civilian address, or at least the address of civilian relatives—and from there I could determine his current whereabouts. Salzberg likes the sauce pretty good, and on the promise that I would drop a bottle around one of these nights, he agreed to do what he could, adding that it would probably take a day or two. I had hoped to have the information in time for the Eugene trip, but he'd said that there was no way he could get to the files before midday tomorrow; I had had to be content with that.

I finished packing my bag, and then went in and soaked in a tubful of hot water for a while. I put on a fresh suit, and some whorish cologne just for the hell of it, and decided I presented a respectable enough image when I looked the package over in the bathroom mirror.

There was a delicatessen over on Union which I frequented regularly, and I stopped in there for some supper. Then I drove out toward the beach, chewing chlorophyll tablets to get rid of the taste and odor of garlic sausage. I felt like a shy kid on his first big date, apprehensive and yet filled with a tingling sort of excitement; it was somehow kind of nice to feel that way again . . .

38

Five

The Golden Door was a neighborhood cocktail lounge, but it was that kind of quiet, sedate, well-mannered place where you could take a wife or a mistress with equal freedom. Beyond the gold-painted door which gave it its name, there was a long narrow room with a bar on the right and some low tables on a raised section to the left. At the far end, the room widened like the bulb on the end of a thermometer into a sunken circular area; in there were a couple of kiln-type fireplaces made out of white brick, extending to the ceiling, and some wall nooks and booths where you could have plenty of privacy. The décor was gold and brown, and they kept it relatively dark with diffused amber lights in the walls and ceiling.

I arrived a few minutes before nine, and Cheryl was not there as yet. I sat at the bar and drank a beer and watched the door. I kept going over in my mind what I was going to say to her; I wanted it to be just right, completely open, completely honest.

A beer-company clock over the backbar said that it was 9:02 when she came in through the door.

She stopped when she saw me, holding a small black purse in front of her at the waist. She was wearing a suede coat and she had a dark scarf tied over her hair. I stood up and went to her, and we looked at each other like two timid children in a dark playground. I said, "Do you want to take one of the booths in back?"

She nodded, and we went along parallel to the bar and down the cement steps into the circular area. There was not much of a crowd this early on a week night, and we found a place at the far end, before one of the fireplaces.

A waitress came around and I asked Cheryl what she wanted; it was a gimlet. I ordered another beer, and the waitress went away. Cheryl took off her coat and unknotted the scarf, tossing her head slightly; the right side of her face was to the wood fire in the brick kiln, and the flickering light gave her hair the impression of burning, like the streak of red-gold fire a setting sun puts across the surface of a clear-day ocean. She wore the same white-and-lavender sweater she had had on that afternoon.

Our drinks came quickly. Cheryl raised her glass and looked at me directly for the first time, over the rim of it. I stared into her eyes, but it was too dark, even with the fire, to see all or any of the things I had seen there earlier. I wanted to tell her she was very lovely, but I did not know how she would interpret it; it was the right thing to say, and it wasn't. You said those same words to a girl you were interested only in seducing, without strings, to a girl you thought no more of than a quick lay, a quick coming, a quick good-bye.

"Well," she asked at length, "do you want to talk about Roy Sands?"

"No," I said honestly, "I want to talk about you."

"You told me you wanted some help in your investigation."

"And you told me you didn't know anything."

"I don't. Roy and I went out together a couple of times, and he came to the house now and then before he and Doug went to Germany. I really don't know him that well."

"All right, then. Now we can talk about you."

"Why do you want to talk about me?"

"I want to know you."

"I see."

40

"I hope you do, Cheryl."

She raised her glass again and drank from it, looking away. "I suppose you're going to tell me you fell in love with me this afternoon. You looked into my eyes there at the door, and you fell in love with me just like that."

"No," I said. "Love at first sight is a lot of hooey. But there's attraction at first sight, a kind of immediate fascination. That's the way I feel about you—and maybe, a little, it's the way you feel about me."

Cheryl was silent for a time. Then, slowly, she said, "We're two strangers—two adults. It's silly, this kind of thing."

She was starting to admit it now, to me as well as to herself. "It's not silly," I told her. "It happens—it happened today. And we don't have to be strangers very long. That's why we're here, isn't it—why I asked you out and why you accepted? The real reason? To become something more than strangers?"

"I . . . don't know. Maybe it is."

"It is, Cheryl. Listen, the simplest way to start it off is by being open and frank with one another. So I'll tell you some things about me. All right?"

She did not answer, and so I went on with it before I could change my mind. I said, "There was this woman, and I was in love with her, the first time I was ever really in love, an old bachelor like me. I asked her to marry me three or four times, but she always said no, with regrets. She'd been divorced a couple of times, and she said she was afraid of trying again, afraid of having to go through another divorce because the first two had been pretty rough on her. But she wanted security, her own kind of security, and I know she would have married me if it hadn't been for my job. She didn't like that, anything about it. She said it was foolish, a losing proposition, a childish fantasy-world of cops and robbers, and she kept after me to give it up. We argued about that, and about some other things, and finally she gave me an ultimatum: the job or her, take your choice. One or the other, but not both—never both."

I got a cigarette out and put fire to it, and I could feel Cheryl's eyes on my face. She would be trying to determine if what I was telling her was straight goods or just a fine old polished line, and that was all right; the answer was the right one.

She said softly, "And you chose your job."

"Yeah," I answered, "I chose my job. I had to do it that way, because even though I loved her, I couldn't quit doing the thing I've done all my life, the only thing I care about doing, the thing that motivates me and keeps me alive."

"This all happened recently, didn't it?"

"Almost three months ago."

"Have you seen her since you . . . made your decision?"

"No," I said. "It wouldn't be any good any more, for her or for me. It's over and it's dead and I keep telling myself that's the best for both of us; but I keep thinking about her and wondering why she couldn't have understood the way it had to be for me. That's all it would have taken, just for her to understand."

Silence formed and built between us. I had a grittiness far down in the back of my throat, but I was not sorry I had told Cheryl about Erika; except for Eberhardt—a close friend on the San Francisco cops—and his wife, she was the only person I had talked to about it. It had been festering inside me like pus gathering in a deep sore.

Cheryl drank what was left of her gimlet, set the glass down, and then turned slightly in her chair to look into the dancing flames inside the kiln fireplace. I smoked, watching her face, the set of her small jaw, the wisp of hair that curled like something spun by Rapunzel on the shoulder of her sweater.

She said, "You must be a very lonely man."

Coming from someone else, those words might have been sharply painful; but from her, they served only in filling me with a sense of warmth and relief. We were all right, I knew that suddenly. It really was going to be fine between us.

I said, "Sometimes. Sometimes I am."

"It's a terrible thing, to be lonely."

"Yes."

"But it's worse to be hurt. Do you know what I mean?"

"I think I do."

"I've been hurt a lot of times, in a lot of ways," she said in a faraway kind of voice. She was still staring into the fire, and the fluctuating shadows were deep on her face, hiding her eyes. "I've been deceived and used and slapped around, always giving and never receiving. If you've been hurt that way, enough that way, you reach a point where you can't take any more hurt, and you'd rather be completely and forever alone than to be hurt even the littlest bit again. Can you understand how that is?"

"Yes," I said.

"It was Tom, my ex-husband, that did it for me. I loved him, I thought he was everything good and sweet in the world, the one really wonderful thing to happen in my life. I gave him everything I had to give or knew how to give— emotionally, physically. I gave him everything and he . . ."

She stopped, abruptly, and held her hands extended, palms outward toward the fire, as if warming them, as if warding off something cold and dark manifesting itself in the canyons of her memory. For a moment I thought she would not go on, and then she began talking again, so softly I had to lean forward to hear her.

"One night, a Saturday, I was sleeping and there were some noises, laughter and some other sounds, and I woke up. It was four A.M. Tom had gone out that night without telling me where and he hadn't come home when I went to bed at midnight. I got out of bed and put a robe on and went to the living room, and he was there—Tom—he was there on the couch with this woman and they were naked and just . . . doing it, there on the couch, very drunk, both of them, and

43

the woman was on top, she . . . she was fat and she was old and she had lipstick and rouge smeared all over her face like a clown. It was . . . it was . . ."

She stopped again, and shuddered, and I wanted to get up and go to her and put my arms around her. But it was not the thing to do, not in this kind of situation, not at this time.

"I moved out that night and went to a lawyer the next morning and filed for a divorce. A friend of mine got me the house on Vicente and I stayed there, and it was very bad for a while. I came close to a breakdown and—other things; but then I got over it, with Doug's help, he was home then, and I was all right. Six weeks afterward Tom and some woman—a different one, I think—were drinking at a place up in Sonoma County and they went off the road coming back and ran into a culvert and killed themselves, both of them. That's why I'm a widow now, instead of just another divorcée."

And that's why you took your maiden name again, I thought. I said nothing, waiting for her to go on.

"I didn't feel anything for him then, when I found out he was dead," she said. "He was . . . just nothing to me any more. I didn't even go to his funeral."

I asked quietly, "How long ago did this happen, Cheryl?"

"Two years now. Two years last October sixth."

"And you've been living alone since then?"

"Except when Doug comes home for the holidays, or on one of his vacation leaves," she said. "We're very close, Doug and I. He's all I have left."

She continued to stare into the fire, and I let her have a few moments with the privacy of her thoughts. The confessions each of us had made as to why we were the lonely people we were had established a bond and a foundation for our relationship, and I knew that when we spoke again, it would be much easier, more natural, between us. That was the way it was. She turned from the fire, and a moment later we were asking questions of each other and there were no hesitations with any of the answers.

44

Cheryl told me she was a waitress-cashier at Saxon's Coffee Shop on 19th Avenue—she made the statement almost defensively, as if I might attach some kind of stigma to her position, the old nonsense about waitresses being dim-witted pushovers—and that Tuesdays were her days off, which was why she had been free today and tonight. She told me she had been born and raised in Truckee, in the High Sierras, but that she and Doug had been orphaned in their teens and had both come to San Francisco shortly after the death of their parents. She had gone to college for a year, liberal arts because that was what all the other girls who had no idea what they wanted out of life had studied, but she had not had the money to continue with her education. For a time she had been a secretary in the Traffic Bureau at Southern Pacific, and then she had been a cocktail waitress, and then she had met this Tom and gotten married, "well, I told you about that, didn't I?"

I filled her in on my own background, my youth in the Noe Valley District, on the fringe of San Francisco's tough Mission; my military and war service in Texas and Hawaii and the South Pacific; my desire to become a cop and my enrollment in the Police Academy; the fifteen years I had spent on the San Francisco police, and the afternoon I had gone out on a homicide squeal and found a guy who had hacked his wife and two kids to pieces with an ax and decided that I had had it with direct police work; the acceptance of my application to the State Board of Licenses for a private investigator's certificate; the lean years since; a little more about Erika, "well, I told you about that, didn't I?"

We smiled at each other across the table, and there was more to say, more to ask. But we had talked enough for one night; part of any relationship is the anticipation of more knowledge, of stronger ties. She sensed it, too, and she said, "I'd better be going now. It's almost eleven, and I have to be to work at eight in the morning."

I nodded. "When can I see you again, Cheryl?"

"You can call, if you like."

"I have to go out of town for a day or two," I said. "I'll call as soon as I get back, and we'll have dinner together, and dancing or a show afterward—whatever you like to do."

"All right."

I helped her on with her coat, and we went through the long narrow section of the lounge and outside. A thick blanket of fog had come in off the ocean, and it was cold and damp on the sidewalk. I walked her to her car, at the end of the block, and it was there that we said good night.

For the first time, but not for the last.

Six

Fog drifted like tattered gossamer through the darkened streets of Pacific Heights. I had to leave my car a couple of blocks from my flat again, and trailing vapors of mist touched my face in a gray, feathery caress as I hurried along the wet sidewalk. They made me feel vaguely chill and apprehensive; it had been a night like this one, a fog like this one, that I had had my belly sliced open during the kidnapping business the previous autumn. The cut, which had required twenty-seven stitches, had scarred thin and white, and even though I had nightmares about it sometimes, I had for the most part been able to bury the terror of that night in my subconscious; but heavy fog, the feel and smell of it, always seemed to release the memory from the mental grave I had dug for it . . .

I reached the foyer of my building and worked the latch-key and stepped into warmth and silence and the dying odors of a corned-beef supper. The anxiety went away as I climbed the stairs, and immediately I felt a return of the high spirits with which I had driven home from the Golden Door. This seemed to be my day for shifting moods, all right. Maudlin in the morning, buoyant at night. I reached the landing at the top of the stairs, and in the semi-darkness there, aimed my key at the lock on my door. Oh, what a difference a day makes—Sinatra hit the nail right on the head. Or was it Tony Bennett who sang that one? Or was it Ella—

And that was when I heard the sounds inside my apartment.

The landing was very quiet, and the scrape of my key at the lock was indistinct, like a rat chittering somewhere in a wall. But the other sounds were graphic, unmistakable—the creak of a loose floorboard, the rustle of clothing, the jangle of coins. There was somebody in there, somebody in my living room, and I turned the key reflexively without thinking about what I was letting myself in for and shoved the door wide.

The knob cracked against a surface of the highboy set against the side wall, and I was two steps into heavy darkness, now thickly silent darkness. I got my hand up, fumbling along the wall to the right of the door for the light switch, and very suddenly a blinding, shimmering white hole appeared in the black fabric of the room, less than ten feet in front of me. Flashlight, I thought, large-cell flashlight— and I threw my left arm up and across my face to shield my eyes, still trying to locate the wall switch with my right hand.

Something came out of the brilliant, diffused aureole of the flash beam, something dark and bulky, and I stumbled awkwardly to the right to get out of the way and collided with the drop-leaf table there, upsetting it. I went down onto my hands and knees, painfully, burning my palms on the worn nap of the carpet; above and behind me the something shattered hollowly against the rose wallpaper. Porcelain shards rained on the backs of my legs like thin, cold hailstones, and I thought: The shit, he threw the reading lamp at me, the goddamn shit.

The flash beam went out, abruptly, and the room once more diminished into a deep-black; the guy, whoever, was running through the flat now, banging into things in the darkness. I got my feet under me and lurched upright, turning back to the wall. I found the switch finally, and pale light from the glass ceiling bowl flooded the room. My eyes ached from the glare of the flash; it took a moment to focus them so

I could see well enough to navigate the cluttered expanse to the doorway on the opposite side, and I could hear him out on the utility porch, trying to get the side door open.

I kicked a footstool out of the way, viciously, and staggered into the kitchen and then out to the porch. The back door was standing wide open. Footsteps pounded down the flight of steep wooden stairs which jutted outward like a prominent rib cage from the old Victorian lady's side wall. I swung through the door onto the pocket-sized platform which serves as a landing for my flat, and a dark man-shape wrapped in a trenchcoat and gloves and some kind of long-billed cap was down at the foot of the stairs; fog and deep shadow helped to camouflage his features, the size and shape of him.

I yelled at him, foolishly, but he was already running along the narrow cement-floored alleyway where the garbage cans and storage bins for my building and the adjacent one were kept. The thought that he might have a gun, or another weapon, did not occur to me until some time later; I clambered down after him, hanging onto the side railing to maintain my footing on the mist-slick stairs, and went into the alley running. The dark figure had already turned the corner, east, at the building front by then; and when I made it up there and through onto the sidewalk, there was no sign of him.

I ran up to the near corner. A car was coming toward me, its headlights magnified by the gray cloak of the fog, but there were four people in it and it was going much too slowly to mean anything. The car passed and I looked up and down the steepness of Octavia; but the area seemed deserted. Whoever he was, he had gotten away clean.

I walked back to the alleyway, trying not to pay any attention to the burning in my lungs from the cold damp air and the exertion. Light spilled into the passage from several flats in both buildings now, and there were anxious faces behind the glass of locked doors and windows. The guy who

49

lives below me, a retired fire captain named Litchak, was standing on his platform, wearing a plaid bathrobe and a sharp scowl. He had a bungstarter in his right hand—a souvenir he had collected somewhere or other.

"What the hell's going on?" he asked me as I started up the stairs.

"I came home and found somebody in my apartment," I told him.

"Sneak thief, huh?"

"It looks that way."

"Figured that might be what it was all about. I heard all the banging around up in your flat, and then him come clattering down the stairs and you after him. He got away, I guess?"

"Yeah."

"Sonsabitches," Litchak said. He made a motion with the bungstarter. "Well, it's too bad the wife had the television blaring away or I might have heard him sooner. If I had, I'd have broken his goddamn head for him."

"Yeah," I said again.

"You think he made off with much?"

"I don't know. I'll check that now."

I started past him, moving up the stairs. He called after me, "Keep your valuables in a safe deposit box, like I do. No sneak thief can hurt you when you've got your valuables locked up in one of those babies."

I reached my own landing and went inside and looked at the door. The lock had been jimmied, hurriedly and unprofessionally; this was the way he had come in, then. I wedged the door closed with a broom handle and a piece of copper wire, and then I went into the kitchen and poured myself a couple of fingers of brandy to ease the jangling of my nerves. When I had that down, I walked through the apartment to see what, if anything, was missing.

Ten minutes later I rang up the Hall of Justice and told a desk sergeant that I had had a prowler, giving my name and

50

address. He had already received one call pertaining to the disturbance, he said, and had dispatched a unit to the area. I could make a report to the investigating officers.

So I sat down on the couch in the living room to wait—and to think about the three items I had found were missing from the flat: twenty dollars in silver dimes and quarters from a wooden bank shaped like a beer keg that I kept on the bedroom dresser; a small case full of cuff links and tie clasps and the like, also from the dresser.

And the sketch of Roy Sands that Elaine Kavanaugh had given me that morning, from the inside pocket of the suit coat I had worn that day.

What the bloody hell?

Twenty bucks in coins and a case of cheap men's jewelry might incidentally interest a sneak thief, but why would one take a rolled-up chalk portrait that was obviously of no real and immediate value—and neglect such easily pawnable items as a clock radio and a radium-dial wristwatch in a nightstand drawer? For that matter, why would a sneak thief take the chance of coming down an open alleyway and up stairs past one door, with three sets of doors and porch windows facing him across the passage? Why would he take the chance of standing fully exposed on the platform while he jimmied open the side door, and of doing it quietly enough so as not to alert any of the neighbors? And why would he choose a time well before midnight, when most people are awake if not still up and around?

The answers were all the same: he wouldn't.

Unless he was not a sneak thief at all.

Unless he was a guy after something in particular, something important enough to make all that risk worthwhile.

The portrait of Roy Sands?

It *had* to be that. I had nothing else that would interest anybody—certainly nothing of special value. I had not had another case in over a month, and that one a simple skip-trace. It had to be the portrait, all right. Coincidence was the only other explanation, and if a lifelong distrust of coincidence was not enough to discredit that possibility, the facts as I saw them *were* enough.

But what made the portrait important enough to steal? A lot of silly and melodramatic ideas crossed my mind—some kind of coded message, a microdot, a concealed masterpiece of some type—and I discarded them all for those very reasons. It had been a simple head-and-shoulders sketch of Roy Sands, and that's all it had been.

Who, then? Elaine Kavanaugh knew I had it, obviously; but because she had given it to me, there seemed to be no conceivable reason why she would want to steal it back again, or have it stolen by someone else. Chuck Hendryx and Rich Gilmartin also knew I had it—and maybe Doug Rosmond as well; he could have spoken to one of them during the day, and that one could have mentioned the portrait. It was likely that Rosmond had known I would be out with his sister tonight, and either Hendryx or Gilmartin could have come over from Marin County and watched my flat and waited until I left, plus a little longer because of the hour, and then broken in.

All of which told me nothing definite. Hell, it did not have to be one of those three at all. At this point, there was simply no way of knowing. But there was one thing I did know, one fact which seemed certain: the theft of the sketch had something to do with the disappearance of Roy Sands, directly or indirectly. And it made that disappearance seem a hell of a lot stranger than it had sounded that morning.

I got up and paced the room, smoking and brooding and getting nowhere, and when the doorbell finally rang I jumped half a foot. I let in two uniformed cops, neither of whom I knew, and showed them around the flat and told them what had happened and what had been stolen, without elaborating on any of my theories. They were polite and solicitous, especially after they found out what I did for a living and that I had been on the cops for fifteen years, and I tried to answer their questions without letting my impatience show through. No, I hadn't gotten a good look at the man. No, I didn't know if he had gotten away on foot or in a car. Yes, I was certain he had been wearing gloves. No, I could not tell them anything more than I already had.

When they were gone—leaving me with the empty assurance that they would do what they could to recover my stolen property—I had another brandy for my nerves and then went into the bedroom and dialed the number of the Royal Gate Hotel. The switchboard rang Elaine Kavanaugh's room and she answered immediately, as if she had been lying tensely awake in the darkness, waiting for the telephone to ring. "Yes? What is it?"

I told her who was calling; then: "Somebody broke into my apartment tonight while I was out. I came home and caught him at it and chased him out, but he got away without me getting a look at him."

I could hear her breathing over the wire. She said at length, "I don't understand. I'm sorry for you, but why did you call me?"

"I have my doubts that this was an ordinary burglary attempt," I said. "The only thing stolen, except for a couple of inconsequential items that seem more like an afterthought than anything else, was that sketch of your fiancé you gave me this morning."

"The sketch? Are you sure?"

"I'm sure."

"But—why would anybody want to steal that?"

"I was about to ask you the same question."

"I have no idea. None at all."

"What can you tell about that sketch, Miss Kavanaugh?"

"Just what I told you at your office. I found it among Roy's things when I was looking through them. That's all."

"Where exactly among his things?"

"Inside his duffel bag."

53

"Was there anything else in there that might connect with the sketch?"

"No, just clothing and such. Do you really think this is important?"

"It might be," I said. "Are you sure he never told you about the portrait in any of his letters?"

"Yes, I'm certain he never mentioned it."

"Then you don't have any idea where he had it done?"

"No."

"Or when?"

"No."

"Or who drew it?"

"No, I'm sorry, no."

"Do you remember a signature? I can't recall seeing one."

"I don't think it was signed."

I shifted the receiver to my left hand. "Did you tell anyone about the sketch? That you'd found it, that you'd given it to me?"

"No, of course not."

"Is your fiancé interested in painting, can you tell me that?"

"Painting? No . . . not really. He likes sports, hunting, *masculine* things."

"Why do you suppose he sat for the sketch, then?"

"Why—to surprise me, I suppose. He knows how much something like that would please me, and I . . . well, I just assumed he had it done for me."

"I see."

"Do you . . . think the theft of the sketch has something to do with his disappearance? *Really* think so?" Her voice had grown very soft, and there was anguish in it now.

"I don't know. It might have."

"But I don't see what! It was just a good portrait of Roy, that's all."

"So it would seem," I said. "Did your fiancé happen to mention in any of his letters how he got along with his buddies—Hendryx and Gilmartin and Rosmond, in particular?"

54

"How he got along with them? I don't understand."

"Was he on good terms with each of them?"

"Well, of course he was. They've been friends for years, all of them. I don't see—"

"I'm just fishing in the dark, Miss Kavanaugh. I'm sorry if I upset you, but I thought you'd want to know about the theft and I did want to ask you some questions about the portrait."

"Yes," she said, "yes, of course. But I . . . oh God, this is so confusing, so frightening on top of everything else. What does it mean? What *can* it mean?"

I had no answer for her. I said, "I'll call you tomorrow from Eugene, Miss Kavanaugh. Maybe some of the answers are up there."

"I hope so. I can't take much more of this waiting, this not knowing."

I said a few gentle parting words, replaced the receiver, and released an audible breath. My watch told me it was almost 1:00 A.M. I thought: She's not going to sleep much tonight, maybe you should have waited until tomorrow to tell her about it. Well, it was too late now; I *had* called her, and she had had nothing to tell me. A lot depended now on what I was able to find out in Oregon; if I ran into a blank up there, there was not much more I could do for Elaine Kavanaugh short of interrogating Hendryx and Gilmartin and Rosmond—and if one of them had stolen the sketch, he would not be likely to admit it to me.

I went out to the utility porch and fussed with the door again, wedging it more tightly shut, and then I walked through the apartment shutting off lights. I looked at the broken lamp in the living room, and finally kicked what was left of it into a corner; I was in no mood to do any cleaning up tonight. In the bedroom I undressed and got into bed and lay there looking up at the dark ceiling, listening to the low moans and creaks and cries of the old building, waiting for sleep to come.

I had to wait a long time . . .

Seven

My flight to Eugene left on schedule at nine the next morning, and it was quiet and uneventful and took something better than an hour. I sat over the wing, tired and vaguely irritable from lack of sleep, and brooded about the theft of Roy Sands' portrait; it got me no further than the brooding I had done the previous night. I thought about Cheryl, then, and that made things considerably better for the duration.

It was snowing a little, not much, when we arrived. I rented a car at Mahlon Sweet Field, because it was the simplest way to do things and in the long run the most economical; and I asked the clerk for a city map and directions to the Western Union office in Eugene proper. He didn't know where it was. I looked it up in the telephone directory and found that it was on Pearl Street, and then located Pearl on the map. I traced out a route that seemed the quickest—and took Highway 99 southeast into the city.

The snow was coming down pretty good now, and there was a lot of traffic. Eventually I reached the downtown area I wanted, left the car in the county parking lot at 7th and Oak, and walked down to Pearl.

The Western Union office had a poorly designed façade, front trim and entrance door set in light green-glass facing material; there were some display candygrams in the front show window, for the holiday season. I entered a large, weakly lighted room with a lobby marked off by counters, the furnishings and transmitting stations behind them giving the impression of age and heavy wear.

A girl about twenty-three, with flaxen hair and a long, tragic face, listened to me tell her who I was and why I was there; she seemed a little awed by my profession. Since the telegrams sent by Sands had gone out after six o'clock, she told me, it would have been a guy named Johnny Saddler —the night man—who had handled the business. She said he came on at six.

I thanked her and left the building, and I could feel her eyes on me as I went through the door and out into the lightly falling snow. It was the old Bogart image, embellished and nurtured by radio and television; they expected you to talk tough and to make cute wisecracks, or at the very least to leer suggestively with one side of your mouth. It stopped being amusing after a while, or even diverting, and became only tedious.

I had noticed that the Eugene City Hall was in the immediate downtown area, and I decided to pay a visit there before I did anything else. It turned out to be a modern affair—wood grille façade made of vertical timbers stained a dark brown—and comprised an entire city block between 7th and 8th avenues, Pearl and High streets; the offices were built around a landscaped court, and the entire area was raised some six to eight feet above the surrounding streets. The police station was on the northwest corner, and you got in there through a solid blue door set into a complete glass storefront.

I spent a little while with a sergeant named Downey—a thin man with an unprepossessing manner—and he said they had been notified by the San Francisco Missing Persons people about Sands and had a file going on him. But they had nothing I did not already know; and they had already questioned Johnny Saddler about the wires, with no helpful results. Downey expressed a willingness to back me up if I needed help in my questioning, since I did not have a valid

58

investigator's license for the State of Oregon. We determined that the goddamn snow was never going to let up, and when I left, it was well past the lunch hour.

I decided I could use a sandwich and some coffee, and I hunched my shoulders against the cold, melting flakes and made my way down to Broadway and along there to a modern shopping mall in the heart of the city. I located a café, and at a small table in the rear I spread the city map open and studied it; then I used their telephone directory to copy down several addresses on the map's margins. Eugene is a relatively small city, and most of the places I planned to check were concentrated in the same general area. Also, and just for the hell of it, I looked up the name Jackson in the directory; there was no listing for a Nicholas, Nick, or N., Jackson.

After I had eaten, I braved the snow again and got to work.

I tried the car-rental agencies first. There were not many, and it didn't take me long to run through them. I came up empty; no one named Roy Sands, or answering Sands' description, had hired a car in the city of Eugene—or at Mahlon Sweet Field—before or after Christmas.

I went around to, or called, the various other transportation outlets—bus, train, airline; but with only a verbal description, and the fact that this was the holiday season, a time of heavy travel, I learned nothing at all. It had only been a shot in the dark anyway.

A check of the new- and used-car lots, on the off-chance that Sands had had enough money to either purchase outright or put a down payment on an automobile, netted me another blank. Business had been relatively slow in the trade, and the managers and salesmen I spoke with assured me they would have remembered anyone named Sands—anyone looking as I described him—making a purchase.

I went to the offices of the *Eugene Register-Guard* next, and spoke with the city editor on the idea that some small incident involving a non-resident might have taken place around Christmas, something that might not have come to the attention of the police. I also wanted to know if the name Jackson had been prominent in the local news for any reason. I was reaching blindly now, but you could never tell when some wild card would give you the break you were looking for. The city editor could not remember anything along the lines I wanted, but he let me look through the newspaper's morgue. I wasted a half-hour there, and came out as empty as I had gone in: no unusual incidents, and the only Jackson an eighty-year-old woman who had died of heart failure.

It was five-thirty by then, and I was cold and tired and wet. I thought about getting a motel for the night, settled for a cup of coffee instead, and returned to the Western Union office to double-check with Johnny Saddler. He turned out to be a young college type, and he wore granny glasses and had a thin grayish mustache like insect larvae laid out to hatch under a very thin, sloping rock.

I let him look at my license, and told him what I wanted, describing Roy Sands; but he was not half as impressed as the girl had been. His eyes said that he was totally uninterested in who I was or why I was there—cops in any form were a drag—and his mouth said that there were a lot of people who came in to send telegrams around Christmas time, he couldn't be expected to remember every one of them even if they sent a dozen wires with money instead of three, sorry I couldn't have been of more help, sir.

"Yeah," I said, and went out of there.

I stood on the wet, neon-lit street outside and thought: Where would Sands go after leaving here? He sent the wires after eight in the evening, and since he hadn't rented a car, it seemed likely he had been on foot. A taxi? A bus? Well, maybe—if he had a specific destination in some part of the city. But if he didn't have, and if he had been on foot and there had been nobody waiting for him, and if he had been lugging that suitcase of his and unfamiliar with the surroundings, he might have thought of getting a place to spend the night.

That was a fair bet—as fair a one as I had been able to come up with yet. I did not much care for the idea of canvassing hotels, motels, boarding houses, and the like in the immediate downtown vicinity, but it would be putting otherwise unproductive hours to good use. As much as I wanted a hotel of my own, and a nice hot bath, I decided to earn my money; I was not up here for rest and relaxation.

I took the area immediately surrounding Pearl Street and then expanded the radius outward in a widening helix, intending on four full blocks in each direction before I gave it up. I went to seven places, gathering discouragement, and then I came to number eight. And there it was.

It was called the Leavitt Hotel, and it was on 5th Avenue not far from the Post Office and the City and County Jail. Snow clinging to window ledges and to the wide old-fashioned porch on the front softened somewhat the eroded face of the tired frame structure; but it—and the darkness—did nothing to conceal the imitation-brick siding of a color we used to call shit-brindle. It was one of these transient hotels, rooms by day, week, and month, an average sort of place that might appeal to salesmen with stringent expense accounts and maybe some pensioners who would live there the year round. The lobby was small, sparsely set up, very clean, but it was an old building and the smell and aura of age was strong in there.

An old guy with white hair as fine as rabbit fur and a face as benign as a saint's was working over a ledger behind the desk. He wore a bow tie and a yellow pencil tucked comfortably behind his right ear, and the glasses tilted out on the end of his nose were as thick as binocular lenses. He gave me a gentle smile as I approached.

I got my wallet out and showed him my license photostat. He blinked a couple of times and ran his tongue over

61

his dentures and looked mildly curious—but that was all. I described Roy Sands, and explained that he had been in Eugene on the twenty-first of December. At the moment, I said, I was working on the possibility that Sands may have stayed a night or two in the downtown area.

"Well," the old guy said, "I guess he did."

"How's that?"

"Sands, you said his name is?"

"Roy Sands, right."

"That description don't tell me much, but I recollect the name. My eyesight's bad but my memory ain't, for a fact." He shuffled over a couple of steps and opened a leather-bound register lying on the counter and riffled through some pages. He found what he wanted, bent closer, peering, and then nodded. "Uh-huh, Roy Sands. Night of December twenty-one. Took a room for a week, one of the singles at fourteen per."

The gods are beginning to smile a little, I thought. I said, "Did you check him in personally?"

"I did."

"Was he alone?"

"Yep."

"Did he seem worried, nervous, preoccupied? Like that?"

"All he seemed was cold," the old guy said. "It was snowing that night, too, and he was all bundled up in a hat and a topcoat and a muffler. He kept hugging himself like he had a chill."

"Did he stay the full week here?"

"Nope."

"How long, then?"

"Only the one night."

"He checked out the next day?"

"Didn't check out at all. He just sort of—disappeared, I guess you could say. But he'd paid in advance, and the key

62

was here at the desk, so it wasn't any of our worry. Except for his suitcase."

"Suitcase?"

"Left it in the room. Maid found it when she went in to clean the next day."

Well, I thought. Well, now. "He didn't come back to claim the case, or call about it?"

"Nope."

"Then—do you still have it?"

He nodded. "Down in the basement."

"Would you mind if I had a look at it?"

"*Through* it, you mean?" he asked shrewdly.

"Yeah, I guess that's what I mean."

"I don't know as I can allow that, since the case don't belong to you . . ."

"I'm working for Sands' fiancée," I said. "She hasn't heard from him since before he came up here, and she's damned worried. They were supposed to be married sometime this month."

The old guy studied me for a time. "Fact?" he asked.

"Fact."

"Can I see that license of yours again?"

"Sure."

I showed it to him, and I could see his lips moving, memorizing my name and address. While he was doing that, I got a card out of another part of the wallet—one of those with my office and home address on it—and handed it to him. He read it over, looked at me out of one eye, and then shrugged. He opened the cash register and put the card in there, under the money drawer, and took out a thick ring of keys. Walking slowly, as if his feet pained him, he came out from behind the desk.

"Come on," he said, "I'll take you down to the basement. I've got to be around while you look through that case, but I can't leave the desk for but a couple of minutes. We'll have to take it up here."

63

"That's fine," I said.

We went through a door and down some dark, narrow steps. The basement was at their bottom, through another door, and it was cold and damp and filled with the kinds of things you would expect to find in a hotel basement: boxes and crates and trunks and some discarded furniture and cartons of accounting stuff and piles of miscellany. The suitcase was off in one corner.

I said as I bent to it, "Is this all he had in the way of luggage?"

"That's it."

"He went away with the clothes on his back, then?"

"Far as I know, he must have."

The case was not heavy. I picked it up and we walked back to the stairs. The old guy clicked off the lights and locked the door again, and we started back up.

I said, "Did Sands have any visitors the one night he was here?"

"None that I know about."

"Make or receive any calls?"

"Nope."

"Did he say anything to indicate where he was going from here, what he planned to do?"

"Not as I can recall. He didn't say much of anything, except to ask for a room."

We came into the lobby again. I said, "Anywhere?"

"Guess so. By the desk there's okay."

I put the case down and opened it, kneeling on the worn carpeting. I emptied it slowly, carefully, putting the contents in neat piles where the old guy could see them. Then I began to sift through the items, methodically.

There was not much. One pair of slacks and one sports shirt, freshly laundered and conservatively cut and colored; a change of underwear and socks; a rumpled gray gabardine suit, a couple of years old and fairly expensive; a necktie of dubious taste, in the current wide fashion; a packet of airmail letters, tied with a rubber band, that were from Elaine Kavanaugh and addressed to Sands at an APO number; and a small leather kit bag containing a band-type razor, an aerosol can of shaving cream, a toothbrush, toothpaste, a bottle of aspirin, a tube of gel hair lotion, a small can of body talc, a spare comb, and a spring case filled with men's jewelry.

I went over the bottom of the case, but there was nothing except some lint and a German pfennig. The kit bag had nothing but the personal hygiene items, and all the clothing pockets were empty. Or I thought they were until I poked an index finger into the slit handkerchief pocket on the suit jacket and came up with a piece of white notepaper folded into a small square. I opened it, and in a neat masculine printing I read:

Galerie der Expressionisten
Blumenstrasse 15

The old guy was watching me from behind the desk. "What you got there?" he asked.

I showed it to him.

"Looks like German," he said.

"Uh-huh."

"Mean something, does it?"

That was a good question. I was thinking about the stolen sketch of Roy Sands, and wondering if Galerie der Expressionisten was an art gallery, and if it was, whether or not there was a connection between the two. "Do you mind if I keep it?" I asked the old guy.

"Well, it rightly belongs to this Sands fella."

"Yeah."

"But I don't see no harm in you copying down what it says there, long as you put the original paper back where you got it."

So I copied the words onto a piece of hotel stationery and put that in my wallet, and then I packed everything back into the case and the old guy and I made another trip down to the basement. When we came back up I put a five-dollar bill on the counter. "For your time and help," I told him.

"I'd rather not, you don't mind," he said. "If I take money from you, it'd put a bad taste in my mouth—kind of like I was accepting bribes or doing something unethical."

I said I understood, and we looked at each other the way a couple of guys will once they've decided they comprehend and approve of one another. We shook hands, and he went back to his ledger and I went back to the cold, wet snow falling across the night.

I picked up my car at the county lot and drove out toward the University of Oregon campus and found a nice-looking motel. I checked in there and called the Eugene police department and told Sergeant Downey what I had found at the Leavitt Hotel; he said he would look into it a little further and that he would contact me if he learned anything more.

I put in a call to the Royal Gate Hotel in San Francisco, and Elaine Kavanaugh was in her room. "I've been waiting and waiting for you to call," she said when I identified myself. Her voice was very tense, and I had the impression she was holding her breath. "Did you find out anything?"

"A little," I said. I told her all the places I had covered, and I told her about the hotel and the suitcase. She was silent for a long moment; then, in a small voice, she said, "It doesn't look very good, does it?"

"I don't know," I answered. "We don't have enough information to do any speculating."

"He wouldn't have left his things in that hotel room unless something had happened to—" She broke off, and I could hear her take a tremulous breath that was almost a sob. "I'm afraid," she whispered. "I'm very afraid."

There was nothing for me to say to that; any words I

66

could have come up with would have sounded forced and tenuous. I let several seconds pass, a coldness on my shoulders, and then I said, "I don't know what this means, if anything, but I found a piece of paper in the pocket of your fiancé's suit—the one in his suitcase at the hotel here. It had the name of a gallery printed on it, and an address that was obviously German—fifteen Blumenstrasse."

"Gallery? You mean an art gallery?"

"I'm not sure."

"Well, what was the name?"

"Galerie der Expressionisten," I said.

"I've never heard of it. What city is it in?"

"There was none listed on the paper."

"Do you think this gallery has something to do with the portrait of Roy? Do you think it means anything?"

"It might. I don't know."

"Roy disappeared for *some* reason. Maybe . . . well, maybe the gallery and the portrait are mixed in somehow. Mightn't that be possible?"

"At this point anything might be possible, Miss Kavanaugh," I said, and sighed inaudibly. I wanted to tell her that rhetorical questions, even though we all indulge in them from time to time, served no real purpose; but I thought that if I did, it would sound cruel. "Do you want me to check around up here another day?"

"Is there any more you can do?"

"Not really. I've covered everything I can think of."

"Then I suppose you'd best come back to San Francisco."

"Do you want me to come by your hotel when I get in?"

"Yes, I think that would be a good idea."

We said good-bye, and I went over to the motel coffee shop and ate a hot dinner and drank some hot coffee to go with it. A long soak in the bathtub and I was ready for bed. I buried myself between the warmth of fresh sheets and a quilted comforter, but for the second night in a row sleep came slowly, reluctantly. A nonsense thing kept running around inside my head:

The time of Sands is running out, the shifting, whispering, vanishing Sands . . .

Eight

The shuttle bus from San Francisco International Airport pulled in to the Downtown Terminal just before twelve the next day. I picked up my overnight bag, went across the street to the parking garage where I had left my car, and locked the bag in the trunk. Then I walked over and down to Powell Street, past the skin-flick houses and the porno bookstores—the new San Francisco, the decadent one, the ugly one. On Powell, I cut across the narrow street in front of one of the few remaining cable cars and entered the Royal Gate Hotel.

This was old San Francisco, vanished San Francisco, a part of the glorious and spirited city that had risen from the ashes of one of the world's greatest tragedies. It was an unostentatious twelve-story building which had once numbered the likes of J. P. Morgan, Louis Bromfield, and Lillian Russell among its many distinguished guests—and had never forgotten them. The quiet, spacious lobby had been modernized just enough to keep it fashionable, but without losing any of its gentility. If you were a native of The City, coming into the Royal Gate Hotel, you felt a little sad, a little wistful, for the things that once were, the traditions—such as the chattering, lurching, magnificent cable cars—that were one by one being returned to those ashes which they had survived or from which they had been reborn. It was that way for me.

I asked an elderly desk clerk, who might very possibly have carried the bags of Thomas Edison or Florenz Ziegfeld in his youth, for Miss Kavanaugh's room; he told me politely that he would have to ring to find out if she would see me, and I gave him my name and waited while he had the switchboard call her. When he had her confirmation, he directed me to the elevators and told me Miss Kavanaugh was in 1012.

I rode up with a uniformed operator, another vanishing breed, and got off and walked through velvet plush past gold inlaid mirrors and rococo furnishings to 1012. Elaine opened the door immediately to my knock, and I went into a large room done in soft blues and dark wood, with a double bed and a writing desk and three chairs and a low, comfortable-looking divan. There was no television set, and that told you something right there.

Elaine wore a beige wool dress, simply cut, and a single strand of cultured pearls at her throat. She was not wearing the silver-rimmed glasses she had had on in my office, and her brown eyes were tired and faintly bloodshot—very probably from a lack of sleep. A vague smokiness seemed to be clouding the textured translucence of her skin, as if some inexplicable form of pollution had begun to consume her from within.

We said perfunctory amenities, and she motioned to one of the chairs and took another one for herself and we sat facing each other with a glass-topped table between us. She had her hands folded on her knees and her knees drawn tightly together, the way she had sat in my office. Her head was erect, chin up, and I could see the cords in her slender throat, the faint pulse beating in its soft white hollow.

"Well," she said with a certain firmness, "I've been thinking about things, and there doesn't seem to be anything more you can do over here."

"Over here?"

"I'd like you to go to Germany," she said.

I blinked at her. "What?"

"Germany. To Kitzingen."

"For what reason?"

"To find out about that gallery and that portrait of Roy. To find out if they have anything to do with his disappearance."

"We don't know that the gallery is *in* Kitzingen," I said. "It could be anywhere in Germany. And we don't even know that it's an *art* gallery. I had planned to check on that today by phone—"

"You don't need to," she said. "The Galerie der Expressionisten is an art gallery, and it is in Kitzingen. I called overseas information early this morning, and there was a listing for it."

"Then we can contact the gallery by telephone."

"I did that, too. I had to have something to do with myself, and so I placed a call to Germany and talked with a man named Ackermann; he owns the Galerie der Expressionisten. He spoke English—very good English."

"What did he have to say?"

"He'd never heard of Roy," she answered thinly. "And he'd never heard of the portrait, at least he said he hadn't from my description."

I rubbed the back of my neck. "I see," I said. "Well, why do you want me to go to Germany, if that's the case?"

Her eyes were steady on my face. "I think it's very strange that anyone would want to steal that portrait, and because it *was* stolen, it must mean something to somebody. Don't you agree?"

"Yes," I admitted.

"Well, Roy had the sketch and he had the address of the gallery, too, and now he's missing—that all could be important, somehow, we don't know that it isn't. You can't tell much by talking to someone on the telephone, and anyway, there are other places you might be able to go if you were over there. If that sketch means something in terms of Roy's disappearance, maybe you can find out what it is in Germany."

"Your fiancé vanished on this side of the Atlantic, Miss Kavanaugh."

"I know that, for God's sake, but the portrait must mean *something*, and we don't have any other clue, do we?"

"No, we don't."

"Well, then?"

"Do you realize how much it would cost you to get me over to Germany and back again?"

"I told you before, I don't care how much anything costs. Don't you understand, finding Roy is the only important thing—nothing else is important, not money, not anything!"

"All right, Miss Kavanaugh, take it easy."

"Will you go to Germany for me?"

"Are you sure that's what you want?"

"Yes, I'm sure, I'm very sure."

I thought: It may be a waste of time and money, but her arguments are valid enough: a connection between that portrait—the theft of it—and Sands' disappearance might very well exist, and the connection could conceivably be found in Germany. One thing is sure: both are damned odd, and both need explanation. You can't just walk out on her now, she's half frantic and she's got nobody else and it's her money after all; you owe it to her for her faith and her investment, you owe it to yourself for what happened the other night.

I said, "Then I'll make the trip for you," and gave her a little smile to let her know I was on her side all the way.

She nodded, and relief was apparent on her pale face. "How soon can you leave?"

"Probably tomorrow sometime," I said. "I'll have to make arrangements."

"Will you need more money, for tickets or anything?"

"Well, I'll have to get some traveler's checks."

She came quickly to her feet and went to where her purse

72

was on the nightstand and got a checkbook out of there. She sat on the edge of the bed. "Five hundred dollars—will that be enough for right now?"

"More than enough."

She wrote very fast and tore the check out and brought it to me. I put it away in my wallet. "I should be going now," I told her. "There are a lot of things I have to do."

"Yes, of course."

"I'll let you know later today what sort of flight schedule I can work out."

"That's fine."

We went to the door and got the farewells said, and I left her there alone with the kind of thoughts you should never be alone with. And as I rode down in the elevator, I realized the nature of that inexplicable pollutant which had clouded her skin with such inner grayness.

It was fear—raw and desperate fear.

There was one envelope in my office mailbox, and my answering service reported no calls in the day and a half I had been away. I put on coffee and opened the valve on the steam radiator and sat down to open the envelope. It was an advertising circular from a mail-order house in New Jersey that specialized in stuff like handguns and balanced Indonesian throwing knives with double-edged blades. Some business enterprise—and some laws to sanction it. I put the circular away in the wastebasket and pulled out the telephone book and set about booking airline accommodations to Germany.

It took a little time, but I managed to arrange a seat on a direct polar route flight from San Francisco to London, leaving the following afternoon at three. From London, I would take a connecting flight to Frankfurt. Kitzingen, it turned out, was some one hundred kilometers south, on the Main River, and I would have to rent a car and drive down there from Frankfurt.

When I had all of that set up, I dialed Cheryl's number and there was no answer. Well, that took care of that for the moment. I sat back and lit a cigarette, and the telephone rang.

It was Chuck Hendryx, wondering if I had gotten back from Oregon yet and if I had learned anything of import. I told him about the hotel, and about the suitcase. He said, "I don't like the looks of it. Roy wouldn't just leave his stuff in that hotel unless he'd gotten into some kind of jam—a bad one, you know?"

"Yeah."

"Have you got any ideas?"

"Not really."

"Well, what do you do now?"

"I go to Germany," I said.

"Germany? What for?"

"Because Elaine Kavanaugh wants me to."

"I don't see the point," Hendryx said. "Wherever Roy is, it sure as Christ isn't Germany."

"No," I said, "but we're dead-ended in Oregon and San Francisco. We've got nothing at all to work on. There's an outside chance I may find something over there."

"Like what?"

"Like whether or not that portrait of him means anything," I said, and I told him about the theft of it from my apartment.

The only reaction I got was: "Who the hell would want to steal a thing like that?"

"I don't know. Somebody seemed to want it—and badly."

"It couldn't be valuable, could it?"

"I don't see how."

"Then stealing it doesn't make any sense."

"Not much seems to in this thing."

"Yeah."

I threw him a soft curve. "What do you know about the Galerie der Expressionisten?"

"The what?" he said. Some pitch.

"The Galerie der Expressionisten. It's an art gallery in Kitzingen."

"I never heard of it. Why?"

"The name came up, that's all."

"Is that where Roy had the portrait made?"

"Possibly. That's one of the things I'll be checking."

"Well, I hope you find something that leads to Roy. I just don't see how that sketch can tie in, but I hope it does if it turns him up. Keep in touch, right?"

"Sure."

So my questions had gotten me nothing at all. I had not really expected them to; if Hendryx—or Gilmartin or Rosmond—had stolen the portrait, they would be on guard against possible slips. The thing was, I could not really envision any of them doing it. There just didn't seem to be any logical reason why one of the three would want to run heavy risks to get his hands on a portrait of his best friend.

That started me thinking about this Nick Jackson again, and I rang up my friend Salzberg at the Presidio. He had the information for which I had asked. Jackson had been born in Salem, Oregon, was divorced, and had no permanent civilian residence; but his widowed mother still lived in Salem, and a brother, Dave, resided in Portland.

I spent the next half-hour on the phone long-distance to Salem and Portland, feigning an old friendship with Jackson. I learned that he was still stationed on Okinawa—but that he had come back to the States for Christmas, returning on the fifteenth of December. He had arrived in Oregon, with a WAC nurse on his arm, on December 24; he and the nurse had gone to San Francisco from Hawaii, the mother told me, and the two of them had been touring the coast, since the WAC was from Georgia and had never been west of the Mississippi until now. Jackson had stayed with Dave and his family in Portland until six days ago, and then he and the nurse had left to do some more touring. His leave

75

was up on the twenty-fifth of the month, and he was scheduled to return to Okinawa, via Hawaii, on the twenty-fourth —flying out of Portland on that date. As to where Nick Jackson had been at the time Roy Sands disappeared, and where he was at the moment, neither mother nor brother could tell me.

I swiveled my chair around and stared out the window for a time. None of what I had learned about Jackson had to mean anything, of course, but it was considerable food for thought—especially because San Francisco had been Jackson's first stateside stop, and his whereabouts between the fifteenth and twenty-fourth of last month were unaccounted for. Depending upon what I learned in Germany, I would have to decide whether or not to fly up to Portland when I returned. In the meantime, Jackson remained on my mind; and he had plenty of company there.

I went into the alcove and rolled out the stand with my portable typewriter on it. For the next half-hour I worked out a report for Elaine Kavanaugh on my investigation thus far, making a duplicate for my files. When I had that finished, I tried Cheryl's number again; there was still no answer.

I notified my answering service that I was leaving for the day, and that I would not be in for several days hence. Then I turned off the heat and started across the office to get my overcoat. Before I reached the coat tree, the door opened and Rich Gilmartin came in.

"What's the word," he said. The corners of his mouth and his silky Continental mustache were pulled up in a glad-hand grin. He wore corduroy trousers with a knife crease and a leather jacket lined in thick white fur.

"How are you, Gilmartin?"

"No kicks. I had to come in to the Presidio today, and so I thought I'd stop by and see if you were back."

"I came in this morning."

"Find out anything in Eugene?"

Well, I thought, let's do it all over again and see what

76

happens. So I did it all over again—relating what I had discovered in Oregon and then going into the theft of the sketch—and nothing happened. Gilmartin possessed a good poker face, and he maintained the same expression throughout. He had no idea why anybody would want to steal the sketch, it had looked like nothing more than a simple street-artist's work to him—was I sure that whoever had broken into my flat was after that specifically? He had never heard of the Galerie der Expressionisten, he said; art galleries were definitely not his bag. And he echoed Elaine's and Hendryx's sentiments that the abandoned suitcase did not look very good for Roy Sands.

When I told him I was leaving for Germany the next afternoon, he said, "What do you figure to find over there?"

"More than I've been able to find here, maybe."

"You're the detective, baby. Locating Roy is the main thing, and if you think you can do that in Germany, you must know what you're doing."

I thought there might be some irony in his voice, but I wasn't sure and I let the remark pass. "What can you tell me about a man named Nick Jackson?" I asked him.

He had nothing to tell me about Jackson—at least nothing that I did not already know. Gilmartin knew of the trouble between Jackson and Sands—he made a couple of obscene references to Jackson's sexual proclivities—and said that as far as he knew, the feud between them had ended with the capture of the men who had actually been responsible for the black-marketeering. Jackson had left the Presidio six months after that, and Sands had not mentioned his name since in Gilmartin's presence.

I got out a fresh cigarette, and I thought of something I had neglected to ask Hendryx. Gilmartin could supply the information just as well. I said, "There's a friend of yours— of Sands—still at Kitzingen, isn't there? MacVeagh, something like that?"

"Yeah, Jock MacVeagh."

"Will he give me a hand while I'm over there? I'm going in cold."

"If he can," Gilmartin said. "Jock's a good cat."

"How do I get in touch with him when I get there?"

"Just tell the main gate sentry you want MacVeagh, in the quartermaster's office. He'll get you there."

"It might be a good idea to send him a wire to let him know I'm coming," I said.

"It probably would. If you're leaving tomorrow, you won't get into Germany until sometime Saturday. Could be Jock's got a little piece lined up off Larson for the weekend."

"How would I address the wire?"

He told me and I went to the desk and wrote it down. He said, "It looks like you've got some work to do, so I guess I'll shove off. Unless you could stand a belt or two."

"Some other time, maybe."

"Yeah, sure. Well, hang loose, baby."

When he was gone, I sat down at the desk and composed a wire to Jock MacVeagh and called Western Union to have it sent off immediately. Then I put on my overcoat, locked the office, and went down to my bank—one that stays open till six on weekdays—to do something about the check Elaine Kavanaugh had given me . . .

Nine

When I got to my flat, there was no mail, no further evidence of illegal entry, and no beer in the icebox. The kitchen contained a faint odor, the origin of which turned out to be a bowl of stew I had cooked but not eaten four days previous. I had forgotten to refrigerate the damned stuff, and it had some kind of gray-green substance over the surface of it. I threw it into a garbage bag and took the bag down the rear stairs to the trash can, wedging the door shut again with the broom handle and the copper wire when I came back up.

You need a keeper, I thought, that's what you need. To clean out this cage once in a while.

In the apartment, I called Cheryl's number another time, and on this occasion I knew intuitively that she would be home. I sat on my unmade bed, listening to the circuit noises and looking at the soiled sheets and the piles of laundry strewn around the bedroom. A goddamn keeper, all right. I wanted a cigarette and gave in to the desire, and in my ear there was a click and her voice said, "Hello?"

"Hi, Cheryl," I said. "How are you?"

I did not have to tell her who it was this time. She said, "Fine. And you?" and her voice was soft and warm.

"Fine. I got back into town earlier this afternoon and tried to call you then, but there was no answer."

"Doug and I were shopping at Stonestown," she said. "Did you find out anything about Roy?"

"Nothing encouraging."

"It's a terrible thing when someone you know just disappears like that, for no reason."

"Yeah," I said. "Listen, Cheryl, I'm leaving for Germany tomorrow. Sands' fiancée seems to think there might be a clue to what happened to him over there. I don't know when I'll be back—just a few days, I think—and I was hoping you'd be free tonight."

"Oh," she said, "I have to work."

I tried to keep disappointment out of my voice. "Tonight of all nights."

"I'm sorry," she said. "I work evenings three times a week, and this happens to be one of them. I wish it wasn't."

I liked the way she had said those last words. I asked, "Well, how's the food out at Saxon's?"

"Fairly good, for a coffee shop."

"Maybe I'll come out for a steak tonight."

"I'd like that, but . . . well, the owner doesn't take kindly to employees having personal discussions while they're working."

"I guess it wasn't such a good idea."

"I hope you understand."

"Of course. Can I see you when I get back from Germany?"

"Yes," she said.

"It's a date. Do you like Russian food?"

"I'm not sure I've ever eaten any."

"I know a place. I think you'll enjoy it."

"It sounds very nice."

"Cheryl—"

"Yes?"

"I've thought of you often since Tuesday night."

"Have you?" Her voice was softer.

"Yes. I just wanted you to know that."

There was a moment of silence that was not in any way

awkward. She said then, "I think I'd better go now. I have to be to work at six."

"I'll call you as soon as I get home."

"Please do."

I paused. "Is your brother there, by any chance?"

"Yes, he is. He's been wondering about Roy, and I know he wants to talk to you. Just a moment."

Doug Rosmond came on immediately and asked me about Oregon. For the third time that day I recounted my trip to Eugene and explained about the theft of the sketch of Roy Sands, and for the third time the reaction was typically innocent: dismay at my discovery of Sands' suitcase in the transient hotel, incredulity at the theft of the sketch, which Rosmond said Chuck Hendryx had mentioned on the phone as being "a pretty good likeness, probably done by one of those sidewalk artists." He had never heard of the Galerie der Expressionisten and wondered where I had gotten the name.

"It was on a piece of paper among Sands' effects," I said. "It's an art gallery in Kitzingen."

"Why would Roy have the name of an art gallery?"

"That's a good question, especially after the theft of the portrait."

"Do you really think this portrait has something to do with his disappearance?"

"It might," I said. "That's one of the reasons I'm leaving for Germany tomorrow."

"Germany? You mean Elaine Kavanaugh is sending you all the way over there?"

"That's right."

"That seems like a hell of a shot in the dark."

"Maybe it is, but it's about all we've got left."

"You think you can find out about the portrait over there?"

"That's what I'm hoping."

"I guess Elaine is getting desperate, and I don't blame

her. If I were in her place, I'd probably have you do the same thing. It's better than just sitting around, waiting."

"That's for certain."

Rosmond wished me luck, and I told him I would be in touch—unnecessarily, because of Cheryl—and we said a parting. I went into the living room and stood at the bay window and looked out through the curtains at the approaching darkness, the subtle transformation of chill bright gray into ebon black. The sharp winter wind blew eddies of dust in a series of miniature tornadoes along the gutters, slapped at the glass with the thin, cold fingers of a crone.

But I was thinking of Cheryl, and that made it a very nice evening in all respects.

The telephone was ringing.

And ringing and ringing.

I pushed my way up through the folds of a deep, warm, comfortable sleep—the first good rest I had had in days. The bell was strident, demanding, in the darkness of the bedroom. I lay quietly for a moment, reluctant to let go of the warmth and the comfort, waiting for the bell to stop. It kept on ringing. I lifted my left arm and looked at my watch, and it was twenty past one. Some time of night for a telephone call; and it will be a wrong number, sure as Christ made fools and drunks, it will be a wrong number.

I swung my feet out of bed and stumbled over to the phone, on the dresser where I had put it earlier. I got the handset up to my ear, a little groggily, and muttered, "Yeah? Hello?"

A muffled, neuter voice whispered, "If you go to Germany tomorrow, you're a dead man, mister. And Elaine Kavanaugh is a dead lady. I'm not kidding, mister—you think I'm kidding, you go ahead to Germany and see what happens."

The line buzzed atonally, emptily.

I stood holding the receiver, fully awake now, and I had a ridiculous urge to burst out laughing. A threatening telephone call. For Christ's sake! Pulp detectives got threatening telephone calls in six stories out of ten, they were always getting them. And then the irony left me and I felt a coldness that was born of anger rather than fear settle across my shoulder blades; anger crept up into my throat, too, and forced itself out in the form of several sharp, savage words. I slammed the receiver down and went to the nightstand for a cigarette.

Hendryx? I thought. Gilmartin? Doug Rosmond? One of those three, goddamn it, it almost has to be one of those three, nobody else knew I planned to leave for Germany tomorrow, not unless Elaine or one of them told someone, and that isn't probable. Well, whoever it was has to be the same one who broke in here—

And the phone rang again.

Two in a row, is that it? I made the dresser in two strides and swung the handset up viciously—and Elaine Kavanaugh's voice said in a broken, frightened, liquid rush, "Somebody . . . somebody on the phone . . . he said he would kill me . . . and you . . . oh God, my God, he said he'd kill us both if you went to Germany!"

So that was the way he was playing it. Her first and then me. Cover all bets. One of us would scare off—that was the reasoning, the son of a bitch. I said thinly, "Easy, Miss Kavanaugh, try to calm down."

"But you . . . you don't understand . . ."

"I understand," I said. "I got the same kind of call, just two minutes ago. The same threat."

"For the love of God, *why?*" Her voice had a shrill, cracking edge to it. "I don't understand this . . . I don't know what's happening . . ."

I spoke softly to her for several seconds, getting her calm. When she seemed in control again, I said, "Did you recognize anything about the voice—anything at all?"

"No, it was muffled, disguised." She released a stuttering

83

breath. "Do you . . . think he meant what he said? About . . . killing us?"

"I don't know," I told her. "I don't know what kind of man we're dealing with here—his motivations, anything about the way he thinks. He might be bluffing, and then again he might not be."

"What are we going to do?"

"That's up to you, Miss Kavanaugh," I said tightly. "I'm not particularly brave, but I don't like voices in the night telling me what to do. As far as I'm concerned, nothing's changed. But I don't want you harmed; if you want to call the trip off, we'll do it that way."

"This is all so . . . insane," she said. "Death threats and Roy missing—I don't know what to do, what to think."

"Maybe we'd better just forget the whole thing."

"No. No, we can't do that. I'm . . . afraid, but I have to know about Roy. I have to know where he is, if he's all right."

"Then I'll have to go to Germany as we planned."

"Yes," she said, and her voice broke faintly, as if she had undergone a violent shudder; then, more firmly, "Yes."

"You're certain that's what you want?"

"I'm certain."

Good girl, I thought. I said, "Then it's settled. But I want you to promise me that you'll pack your things and check out of that hotel early in the morning. Will you do that?"

"Where will I go?"

"To another hotel. Any one you like, but make it some distance from the Royal Gate. Register under another name —anything but Smith or Jones. You can call me at my office tomorrow and tell me where you've gone."

"All right. If you think that's best."

"While I'm in Germany, I want you to stay in your room. Don't go out, don't tell anyone—anyone at all—where you are, and don't open your door to anyone but a member of the hotel staff. You can have your meals sent up, and books

84

to read or a television to help pass the time. It'll be hell for a few days, but you'll have to do it. Do you think you can?"

"Yes," she answered, and I believed her.

"You'll be okay tonight. Take a couple of sleeping pills, if you have them, and try to get some rest. I'll do all that's humanly possible to find Roy Sands for you; I hope you can believe in that."

"I can."

"That's fine," I said, "because we've got one thing going for us now, one thing those threatening calls told us for sure."

"What?"

"That there's something damned important to be found out in Kitzingen, Germany."

Ten

It was raining in Frankfurt, Germany.

I had never been able to sleep on airplanes, and when we arrived it was almost seven o'clock in the evening and I had been awake for something like thirty hours, discounting the nine-hour time difference between California and Western Europe. The TWA flight to London, in one of the big new useless 747's, had taken close to twelve hours, and I had gotten entangled with a huge customs line at Heathrow Airport and a lot of red tape because bad weather had socked the place in for two days and all flights were either canceled or well behind schedule. My Lufthansa connection to Frankfurt was delayed two hours, but I had not been able to sleep in the waiting room because of the huge crush of people awaiting departure. Consequently, when I disembarked I was exhausted and irritable and in no damned shape to drive a hundred kilometers in a driving rain on a dark night in a strange country.

I picked up my rental car, a Volkswagen, and a road map, and managed to find my way out of the airport. I drove to the nearest overnight accommodations, a modern American-type motel, and took a room. I thought about calling Elaine to see if she was all right, but I decided to wait until I got into Kitzingen. She had followed my instructions about getting another hotel, and she was now registered as a Miss Elaine Adams in the Argonaut Hotel on California Street; I had talked with her briefly just before leaving on Friday afternoon and she had seemed well in control of the situation. I was fairly certain she would remain in her room, as I had asked, and if she did that she would be okay.

I had a quick and very hot bath, got in between cool sheets, and went to sleep immediately. I slept too heavily to be particularly well rested or refreshed when the eight o'clock call I had requested woke me Sunday morning. It was still raining. I took the road map, and the German language books I had bought in San Francisco prior to leaving, into the motel's dining room for the Continental breakfast included in the room price. I located my position on the map and figured out a route south to Kitzingen, and then continued refreshing my memory with the German books; I had had a course in the language as part of my military training, with the Intelligence unit I had been assigned to in the South Pacific, but the years of disuse had pushed most of the words and the grammar far back into my subconscious. The books, which I had begun reading on the flights, had helped a little and I thought I could get by all right.

I paid twenty Deutsche marks for the room and put my luggage into the Volkswagen and set out for Kitzingen. I got lost a couple of times in the rain, and had a bad scare with a truck near Schweinfurt; I was the original babe in the woods, and my nerves were frayed when I reached Kitzingen a few minutes past eleven.

It was a small, attractive town set on a flat plain and surrounded by fertile fields and lush green forests of beech and oak; this was wine country, where they made the tart white Frankenwein in the valleys near Iphofen and Rödelsee to the southeast. The buildings were Gothic and German and Italian Renaissance in design—some with lavish wood studding, some with simple brickwork façades, almost all with rust-colored tile roofs. Here and there were squared or rounded church towers, reaching up into the wet gray sky, and the bells in some of them filled the morning with a resonant summons.

I entered the town proper, crossing the rail tracks connecting Würzburg and Nuremberg. At Der Falterturm, a huge brick tower and carnival museum set in a wide flowered square, I turned to the left and into the center of the village. After ten minutes of searching, I located a hotel—the Bayerischer Hof—on Hernstrasse; there was not much traffic, and I found a place to park on the street and went inside with my bags.

I took a room on the top floor, and from the window I could look out at the narrow gray waters of the Main River, the tree-studded opposite bank, the green and glistening land spreading out to the south. I spent a few minutes unpacking, and then I went downstairs and asked the desk man—who spoke excellent English—to arrange a transatlantic call to San Francisco for five that evening; that would make it about 8:00 A.M. California time and I would not be frightening Elaine Kavanaugh with a middle-of-the-night call.

This being Sunday, it was a certainty that the Galerie der Expressionisten would be closed—so I decided to look up Jock MacVeagh at Larson Barracks. I asked directions, and the desk man produced a map and pointed out the way.

The base was located to the northwest of the town, and you got to it via the Steigweg, on the other side of the rail tracks. It was a sprawling compound of weathered buildings, with a stoic gatepost sentry at the main entrance. I stated my name and the nature of my business, and it turned out that Jock MacVeagh had left word at the gate that I was to see him in his quarters, this being an off-duty day. The sentry gave me directions, and I found the place easily enough, well toward the rear perimeter of the compound.

It was a large building, without much adornment, divided into private residence facilities for the non-commissioned officers. I located MacVeagh's quarters and rapped on the door, and a moment later it swung wide.

He was a big, red-faced Scotsman with huge hands and a wedge-shaped torso and eyes as black as a peat bog at midnight. Whiskey-broken veins etched the skin on either side of a somewhat battered nose, and he had the kind of wide mouth that would be quick to smile, quick to set in angry belligerence. His jaw was like a clefted granite bluff. But he was aging, too; you could see it in the lines and tributaries of his face, the roundness of his belly, the receding hairline, the faint liver spots among the dark black hairs on the backs of his hands.

I introduced myself, and the mention of my name brought a flashing grin like a neon sign coming on. He had an iron grip, but he did not try to prove anything with it. "I've been expecting you," he said. "I figured you'd be in last night."

"Well, I made Frankfurt," I told him, "but it was late and I was too tired to drive down."

"No sweat. Come on, I'll pop you a beer."

We went inside and his quarters were small and neat and orderly, the bed made according to regulations and his clothes picked up and hung away. He had some German-manufactured stereo equipment set up on one side of the room, and a lot of color and black-and-white photographs of women—interspersed with German beer and liquor signs—on the walls. He got a couple of bottles of Löwenbräu out of a small cooler and opened them and gave me one. We sat across from each other at a small dining table.

MacVeagh said, "I had this little *Fräulein* set up in Stuttgart for the weekend, but when I got your wire about Roy having disappeared, I said to hell with it. A buddy's more important than a piece of tail any day, and besides that, she'll be around next weekend; they always are."

I had some of the Löwenbräu, and it was cold and rich and very good; the Germans brew the best beer in the world. I watched MacVeagh over the tilted bottle, and I thought: He's one of the good-time boys, too, like Hendryx and Rosmond and Gilmartin—one of the handsome ones, the popular ones, the ones with the right word, the right phrase, the right line; the lovers, the cocksmen, with the

90

world their bedroom and the bed seldom empty and seldom silent. But now they're fast approaching middle age, and some of their appeal is fading, and some of their virility perhaps, and they can see the end now; they can see the wrinkles and the arthritis and the dentures and the shriveled glands; and they can see, too, the scornful looks and hear the mocking laughter of the daughters of the girls who once flocked to them. That glimpse of the future terrifies them, haunts them, gnaws at them, becomes almost an obsession, and they need constant reassurance of their prowess, constant reaffirmation of their attractiveness—running scared, telling more lies, bragging more and exaggerating more, laughing louder and longer and increasingly more hollowly. And each time they go searching for a woman, they're filled with the same terrible dread: Can I still attract the young ones, the pretty ones? And when they find that they can, if they can, the attendant dread is always there and always the same as well: Suppose, this time, I can't get it up; suppose, this time, I can't perform?

Every man around my age has harbored some fears of failing virility, and I was no exception; but I had never been a cocksman, never wanted to be one, and when I saw guys like MacVeagh and the rest, I was thankful for that. When you took sex away from them, you took away their main purpose—and without purpose, no matter what form it takes, what more can you do except simply to vegetate? That was one particularly frightening hell I did not think I would have to face.

I set the sweat-beaded bottle down on the table. "The pickings must be pretty good over here," I said, because that was what MacVeagh wanted to hear.

He grinned, and his black eyes sparkled. "The best," he said, nodding emphatically. "Listen, if you're interested, I can fix you up with something hot and willing right here in Kitzingen. Guaranteed, baby—the original German Valkyrie."

"Well, if I can find the time."

"Yeah," MacVeagh said, and his expression sobered. "Roy. Why don't you fill me in on the details? All I know is what you said in your wire."

I filled him in on the details, leaving out the threatening telephone calls to Elaine and me and skipping lightly over the theft of the portrait. He listened attentively, a frown digging horizontal trenches in the red-hued skin above his eyebrows.

"I don't much like the sound of it," he said. "Roy was gone over the Kavanaugh chick, and if he hasn't contacted her in three weeks, something must have happened to him. You really figure there's some kind of connection between Kitzingen and him disappearing in Oregon?"

"That's why I'm here—to find out."

"I don't get this portrait you told me about. Hell, Roy isn't the kind of guy to pose for a goddamn picture."

"He never mentioned it, then?"

"Christ, no. We'd have kidded him into the next century."

"Do you have any idea who might have drawn it?"

"Not hardly."

"What about this gallery here in Kitzingen?"

"What was the name of it again?"

"Galerie der Expressionisten."

"I didn't even know it existed."

I got out my cigarettes and offered MacVeagh one, and we sat smoking and drinking from the bottles of Löwenbräu. You could hear the gentle skittering of the rain on the building roof, and watch it flowing in streaked silver patterns down the panes of the window nearby, like tears on the smooth shining face of a child.

I said, "How did Sands get along with his buddies? Rosmond and Hendryx and Gilmartin, especially."

"Fine. Hell, everybody likes Roy."

"No trouble with any of them while they were here?"

"No. Why—what are you getting at?"

"Nothing in particular," I said. "Do you know an Army major named Jackson, Nick Jackson?"

92

"Name's not familiar. Why?"

"Sands had some trouble with him once. I thought he might have mentioned the name in some context or other."

"Not to me." MacVeagh frowned. "What kind of trouble?"

"It was over a girl," I said, and watched the frown change to a knowing grin. I took the conversation in another direction. "Did Sands spend a lot of time in Kitzingen?"

"As much as the rest of us."

"Any special place?"

"Not really," MacVeagh said, and began chuckling.

"Something funny?"

"Kind of, yeah. I just happened to think about the Dodge City Bar."

"What's that?"

"A *Kneipe*. A dive on the Am Pfuhl, in what passes for whoretown hereabouts."

"Sands used to frequent this place?"

"Hell, no. But he *lived* there for three days."

"I don't get the point."

"There isn't one, really. Roy went on this three-day bender back in October—the end of the month, I think it was. And he picked the Dodge City Bar to do his drinking in, for some reason. Man, what a hole; he couldn't have found a worse place if he'd tried."

"I was under the impression that Sands is a low-key drinker, that he leaves the booze pretty much alone."

"That's right, he does. But he was really juiced this one weekend. I've never seen a guy—any guy—that juiced before or since. He was damn near pickled in alcohol. Funny as hell." He laughed. "Ed Botticelli and me had to go into town to bring him before the C.O. raised a flap. He was supposed to be back on duty that Sunday night, but when he didn't show by next morning, Ed and me requisitioned a jeep and went looking for him. Took us a couple of hours to find him; who the hell would have figured the Dodge City?"

"Why did he go on this bender?"

"Who knows? I tried to talk to him about it once, a couple of days afterward, and he went cold and distant on me. So I dropped it. I guess he just got uptight about something and decided to tie one on."

"Did he usually drink heavily when he was uptight?"

"No. Like you said, he was pretty much of a low-key boozer."

"Did he say anything at all to you while he was still drunk?" I asked. "Like when you first found him, or when you brought him back here?"

"Seems to me he kept repeating the word why, like he was asking a question. 'Why? Why? Why?'—like that."

"That's all?"

"That's the only thing I remember. Listen, why all the interest in a simple bender?"

"Because it seems out of character."

"Hell, everybody does something out of character a time or two in their lives."

"Sure," I said, "but everybody doesn't disappear without apparent reason. Do you have any idea where Sands had been before he went to this Dodge City Bar?"

MacVeagh shrugged. "He was there the whole weekend, like I told you; at least that's what the barkeeper told Ed and me. He'd come staggering in early Saturday night, bought a bottle, and sat off in a corner drinking out of it until he passed out. There are some rooms in the back of the place, over an alley, and the barkeeper and a couple of corporals who were in there got Roy up in one of them to let him sleep it off. The next morning he came down and paid for the room and bought another bottle and started in all over again. It got to be a goddamn ritual until Ed and me came in on Monday—and it's a good thing we did, too, because Roy was almost out of money and they would have dumped him flat in the alley the next time around. It's a miracle he wasn't rolled half a dozen times as it was."

"Did Sands say anything to the barkeeper, or to anyone else?"

94

"We didn't stick around to ask questions," MacVeagh said. "The main thing on our minds was getting Roy out of there and sobered up and back here."

"He go on any other benders after that one?"

"No. He stuck pretty close to base until he left for the States last month."

"Anybody else he might have confided in?"

"He's pretty close-mouthed. If he didn't tell me, it isn't likely he told any of the other guys."

I drained the last of my beer. "Do you happen to remember the exact date this drinking bout took place?"

"Not offhand. Wait a minute." MacVeagh got up and went to where a *Playboy* calendar hung on one of the walls; it was last year's, open on the month of December. He flipped back through it, and then said, "It was the last weekend in October—yeah, Saturday, the thirtieth, through Monday, November one."

I made a mental note of the dates. "How do I find the Dodge City Bar?"

"You planning on going there?"

"I thought I might do that."

"Well, I guess you know what you're doing."

"There's not much else I can do until tomorrow," I said. "There may not be anything in this bender, but it can't hurt to look into it a little."

"If you say so," MacVeagh said. "How's your German?"

"Rusty, but I think I can get by."

"Mine's pretty good. Why don't I come with you tonight? Might be a good idea anyway, since you don't know whoretown and you don't know the *Kneipen*. I haven't got anything else to do, now."

"Thanks, I'd appreciate it," I told him. "I'm strictly a backwoods boy over here."

"I know a place where you can get a pretty good schnitzel," MacVeagh said. "Suppose we have dinner and a couple of beers, and then get around to the Dodge City before it jams up?"

95

"Fine by me."

"You got a hotel yet?"

"The Bayerischer Hof."

"Meet you there at six, in the bar."

"Good enough."

The rain had slackened considerably, I saw as I went out to the Volkswagen; pale blue lines patterned the gray overcast above, like incisions carefully made by a surgeon. There was very little wind. I drove directly back to the Bayerischer Hof, ordered a hot brandy sent up to my room, and drank it lying propped up on the bed, thinking alternately of Elaine Kavanaugh and Cheryl and the inexplicable disappearance of Roy Sands.

Five o'clock came and my call to San Francisco went through. Elaine was fine, bearing up admirably; she had not left her room at the Argonaut Hotel, and she had not been bothered by visitors or phone calls. Her voice seemed faintly listless, but I put that down to the prolonged inactivity, the constant waiting; apathy is just one of the mind's defense mechanisms, and a far better one than screaming agitation. It made me feel better to know that she was unharmed and firmly anchored.

I told her about my talk with MacVeagh and asked her if Sands had ever mentioned the three-day bender; she said that he hadn't, and seemed surprised that he had done a thing like that. He just didn't care for liquor that much, she said, and she could offer no explanation for it. I said that I would check it further, and get down to the Galerie der Expressionisten first thing in the morning, and that I would call her again tomorrow night whether or not I had anything definite to report.

I cut the call short then, to alleviate expenses as much as possible, and went in to shave for my visit to Kitzingen's whoretown.

96

Eleven

MacVeagh was twenty minutes late arriving at the bar in the Bayerischer Hof, which was not particularly surprising; he had struck me as anything but the punctual type. I was on my second bottle of Scheuernstuhl, Kitzingen's personal contribution to the brewer's art; the only other paying customers were two elderly types playing chess and drinking schnapps under an ornate brass lamp in one corner.

I saw MacVeagh come in and raised a hand at him, and he came over to where I was sitting. He was in uniform, a fur-lined greatcoat thrown carelessly over one shoulder; by the three chevrons above the single arc on the sleeve of his blouse, I could see that he was an E-6—a staff sergeant. I had the thought that he had held the non-com rank for some time, and that he would continue to hold it until he retired or perhaps died from one ailment or another. He was not exactly a world beater, and an extra stripe or two would have no special value in the pursuit of his true life's work.

He sat down beside me and I bought him a bottle of Scheuernstuhl and we made a little small talk about nothing much. When the beer was gone, we left the hotel. MacVeagh said, "We can walk to the restaurant I mentioned this afternoon—it's only a couple of blocks—but we'll have to take your car to the Am Pfuhl later on unless you want to shell out for a taxi. I hitched in."

"That's no problem."

We walked to Mainstockheimer Strasse, which paralleled the Main River to the north. There was no rain, but the rifts in the clouds had been sutured with thick black thread; the wind had picked up and it was considerably colder than it had been earlier. The dark, still water of the river appeared frigid, as if it were at the point of freezing solid. You could see the bright clear lights of the houses strung along the opposite shore, and to the east the lighted runways at Harvey Barracks—the Army Air installation which flanked Kitzingen in that direction.

The restaurant MacVeagh steered me to was called Die Vier Jahreszeiten—The Four Seasons—and it was located in an ornately façaded brick building facing toward the river. We managed a table in the crowded main hall, and ordered Wiener schnitzel and green salad and German rye bread and bottles of Scheuernstuhl. The food arrived in a couple of minutes—Teutonic efficiency—and I had to admit that MacVeagh had a valid appreciation of the local cuisine.

Over cigarettes and coffee he said, "Well, what do you think of Germany so far?"

"I haven't seen enough of it to form much of an opinion."

"It grows on you, gets into your blood. I been here eight years now, at Larson and Mannheim and Bad Kreuznach, and I wouldn't go back to the States on a bet. They got good beer, better food, and the best pussy in the world. What more could you want?"

I could think of a couple of things, but I said, "Not much, I guess."

"You married, are you?"

"No."

"Smart boy. I been through the mill twice. American women don't know how to treat a man. But a German chick —well, Jesus, I was shacked up with this one the last time I was in Munich . . ."

So I listened to him tell about the last time he was in Munich, his eyes glowing, and maybe it was the truth and maybe it wasn't; it sounded very good and very false at the same time, so that you had the feeling that even if it was true, he was touching only the very highest points and maybe embellishing those a little. I wondered what he would say if I told him about Cheryl and the way it had been that first time at her house; but then I thought I knew what he would say and I kept my mouth shut and let him talk until he was finished inflating his ego. He let me pay the check and we got out of there.

At the Bayerischer Hof, we picked up my rented Volkswagen and drove south, following the curve of the river, until we came to an old, dark section of the town, near the rail tracks. The sound of a train whistle, low and wistful, punctuated an indication from MacVeagh for a left-hand turn, and I saw by the street sign that we were now on the Am Pfuhl.

It was a short, narrow, twisting street with a considerable amount of pedestrian traffic. Neon bar signs cast surrealistic red and blue and green shadows over the rough brick buildings standing shoulder to shoulder on both sides of the street, and there were black alleyways and small iron balconies at the stories above the pavement. Enlisted servicemen walked in pairs and groups, but seldom alone.

In the second block MacVeagh pointed to a heavy rococo door set between two milky-white globes on tarnished brass arms; black lettering on the lighted globes read: DODGE CITY BAR. "That's it," he said. "Some place, huh?"

"Matt Dillon would be proud."

We went another block, and Am Pfuhl ended at a well-lit thoroughfare. MacVeagh directed me to a spot under a streetlamp, for obvious reasons, and I parked there and locked the Volkswagen. We walked back to the Dodge City.

Inside, there was not much to differentiate it from its brother establishments in two dozen countries around the world. You went down three steps into a dark smoke-filled room with a long bar and tables and booths in the rear.

99

There were red and green lamps on the bare walls, and candles in wine bottles on the tables. Behind the bar were three huge wine casks draped with imitation grapes on wilted vines, and a short, fat barkeeper sporting mutton-chop whiskers and wearing a tattered red coat and a bow tie as wilted as the grape vines.

The place was about a quarter filled, but it was early yet and they would pack them in later on—you had that feeling. Bar girls in low-cut shiny dresses numbered fifteen or twenty, and there was a lot of laughter and a lot of sporadic singing in accompaniment to discordant German rock music emanating from a garishly lighted jukebox. I followed Mac-Veagh up to the bar, and we got some looks from three *Flittchen* painted like Barnum clowns sitting off on our right.

The barkeeper came down and nodded and said, "*Ja, bitte?*"

In German, MacVeagh ordered a couple of beers and then said that he wanted to ask him some questions about a friend of ours, a soldier. The barkeeper started to protest that he didn't have time for talking, saw the way MacVeagh was looking at him, and closed his mouth. He opened two bottles of Scheuernstuhl and set them in front of us. "*Was ist es?*"

MacVeagh asked him if he remembered the American soldier who had been drunk in there about three months ago —the one they had had to keep putting in a room in the back each time he passed out. The barkeeper grinned a little and touched his muttonchops and said that he remembered him very well, yes, and weren't you one of the men who came to take him back to the *Flakgelände?* MacVeagh admitted that he was.

He said, "Did you talk to the soldier while he was drinking in here?"

"Only to sell him another bottle of schnapps," the bar-

100

keeper answered, and shrugged. "He did not want conversation."

"Then he didn't say where he had been before he came here?"

"Not to me."

"Or why he was drinking as he was?"

"No."

"Did he talk to anyone while he was here?"

"No—ah well, perhaps to Sybille."

"Sybille?"

The barkeeper shrugged again. "*Ein Flittchen*," he said.

"Is she here now?"

The guy let his eyes move slowly over the room, squinting against the pall of smoke. He shook his head.

"Will she be in tonight?"

"It is possible. One never knows with Sybille."

I said slowly, in German, "Why do you think the soldier may have talked to her?"

"She sat with him for a time, the first night—Saturday."

"And after that?" MacVeagh asked.

"He sat alone," the barkeeper said. "He sent the girls away when they came to his table. Some soldiers and myself carried him to one of the rooms in back two or three times. Once I had to take him alone."

"Was the soldier drunk when he arrived that first night?" I asked. "Or did he become drunk in here?"

"I think he was not drunk when he came."

"Was he nervous or afraid or angry?"

"He appeared very weary—an old man."

"That's all?"

"I can remember nothing more." The barkeeper glanced over his shoulder, and there were a couple of customers yelling for service at the other end of the bar. His eyes flicked over MacVeagh and me again. "I have no more time for talking now."

"Okay," MacVeagh said. "But you point out Sybille to us if she comes in. We'll be at one of the tables."

"*Ja, ja.*" He turned his back to us and hurried away along the boards.

MacVeagh and I carried our beers to one of the empty tables and sat down, and immediately two of the girls who had been sitting to the right of us at the bar came over. Mac-Veagh looked them up and down with plain contempt—they were nothing for his ego—and said something in German that I did not understand. One of them laughed shrilly, and the other looked offended; they both shuffled away.

A half-hour passed, and the place began to fill up with soldiers and civilians alike, pressing two- and three-deep at the bar. The stale, steam-heated air was bloated with shouts and laughter and the strident electronic discord bursting forth from the juke. I began to get a headache, and there was a tightness in my chest from too many cigarettes and the sour atmosphere. I coughed a couple of times and spat up phlegm into my handkerchief, and I thought: Oh God, not this again.

At the bar in front of our table, there was some kind of commotion. The knot of humanity split into two halves, flowing away, like an amoeba reproducing. Two guys, both of them wearing civilian clothes, one in lederhosen, were shoving at one another, yelling. Then the one in the lederhosen put his back to the bar and hit the other in the stomach, bending him double. He followed up with a looping right hand, and the first guy came windmilling backward, in a direct line to where I was sitting.

I kicked my chair away and got on my feet, turning my body, bracing myself. I caught the guy on my left hip, stopping him cold, and then I put both hands on his shoulders and sent him back the way he had come. He ran into the one in lederhosen, and the two of them went down in a tangle of arms and legs. Two big Germans, bouncer-types, came out of nowhere and scooped the pair off the floor like they were bags of meal and got rid of them through the front door. Somebody shouted in German, and there were some cheers and a round of applause, and an American acid-rock thing came on the juke.

I sat down again and MacVeagh looked at me as if he was seeing me for the first time. "You handle yourself damn nice, buddy."

"Yeah—well."

"You ever in the service?"

"Pacific Theater, Second War."

"Infantry?"

"Army Intelligence."

"Yeah?" MacVeagh said, in a way that told me he was not particularly impressed.

We had another beer, and MacVeagh wanted to talk about the war—he had been a private first on the beach at Normandy; but my headache had steadily worsened and the tightness had grown more painful in my chest, and I did not feel like talking. I was thinking about chucking the whole business for tonight when the ornate door opened and a black-haired girl in a short green dress came down the steps into the room.

The muttonchopped barkeeper saw her and made a signaling motion to MacVeagh from behind the plank. The girl stood looking things over at the bottom of the steps, and MacVeagh got up and waved to her with the same kind of contempt he had shown the two *Flittchen* earlier. She put on a professional smile, paused, and then walked with an exaggerated hip-sway to where we were sitting.

She was maybe twenty-five, lush and ripe now like a piece of fruit at peak season, but it was only a matter of time before the first sweet flesh would turn into blotched and taste-less pulp, rotting and discarded at the base of the tree which had borne her. She had a wide mouth and bovine eyes and, characteristically, round dimpled cheeks literally white-washed with makeup.

103

MacVeagh asked her sharply if she spoke English. Distaste was apparent in his voice.

She bobbed her head vigorously. "Sure, I can good English speak. Christ, yes!"

"Your name is Sybille?"

"You know me?"

"Yeah, we know you," MacVeagh said. "Sit down, we want to talk to you awhile."

"You buy me a drink?"

MacVeagh's mouth twisted, but I said, "We'll buy you a drink, Sybille. What do you want?"

She pulled out a free chair and sat down and pressed her heavy breasts against the edge of the table. She looked directly at me, ignoring MacVeagh. She said, "I drink an gin fizz."

"All right."

"Oh shit," MacVeagh said.

"I'll handle this, Jock," I told him, and his eyes answered, *You know all about handling whores, huh, buddy?* but he did not say anything. He lifted his beer and looked off in another direction.

I got a gin fizz for Sybille and watched her drink a little of it; then I said slowly, "About three months ago, on a Saturday, there was an American soldier in here drinking. His name was Roy Sands. He spent the whole weekend here, drinking and passing out and sleeping it off in one of the rooms out back. Do you remember?"

She smiled, frowned, smiled again. "Oh sure, I remember."

"You were sitting with him at one of the tables, weren't you?"

"For a little time," she said. "Then he wants to be alone."

"Why?"

"To drink the schnapps."

"Why did he want to drink so much schnapps?"

She shrugged. "I think he was unhappy."

"Did he tell you that?"

"No, but his eyes and mouth are unhappy."

"Can you remember anything he said to you?"

"He ask me why did it have to happen."

"Why did what have to happen?"

"*Ich weiss nicht.* I don't know."

"All right. What else did he say?"

"That he wants to be alone. No more."

"Did you talk to him again on Sunday or Monday?"

"No."

"Did you see him at all after that weekend?" I asked her. "Did he come in here again?"

"I never see him any more."

"Do you know of anyone else who might have talked to him?"

"Walter, the barkeeper."

"We've already spoken with Walter."

"Two *amerikanische Soldaten* helped to put him in a room."

"Do you know their names?"

"No."

"Would Walter know their names?"

"Walter does not even know his own name," she said, and laughed.

"Anyone else?"

"*Ich weiss nicht.*"

"All right, Sybille. Thanks."

"You buy me another gin fuzz, huh?"

"Yeah," I said, and I put a couple of D-marks on the table. She smiled wetly. "Thanks, man."

MacVeagh was on his feet. "Let's get out of here," he said to me. "I can't stand this goddamn hole any more."

I nodded and we left Sybille tucking the D-marks into the loose bodice of her dress. Outside, the clean, chill air blowing along the Am Pfuhl was like dry ice in my lungs, and my head throbbed painfully. MacVeagh said nothing, sullenly, as we walked to where I had parked the Volkswagen on the thoroughfare. He had not approved of the way I had handled Sybille, and he thought he had me pegged because of it; I was a slob in his book now, even if I did know how to handle myself. He was even shallower than I had previously thought.

When we got to the car and I had the engine warmed up, I said, "I'm ready to call it a night. You want me to drop you back to Larson?"

"No, it's too damned early. I'll get out at the Bayerischer Hof."

He directed me back there, in clipped sentences, and I put the Volkswagen away in their garage area. On the street in front I said, "I'll let you know if I turn anything on Sands tomorrow—or if there's anything else you might give me a hand on."

"Yeah, you do that," MacVeagh said, and he went away without looking at me again.

I watched him go, and then I coughed and spat phlegm into the street and entered the lobby, listening to the blood pound in my ears . . .

Twelve

Blumenstrasse was a little cobblestoned street in a semi-residential area a few blocks from the Bayerischer Hof, and number fifteen was a dust-colored building with intricate wood-studding from sidewalk to peaked roof. A rounded arch gave on a short vestibule, and above the arch was a small sign lettered in pale blue: Galerie der Expressionisten.

I parked the Volkswagen across the narrow street and sat looking over there for a time. It was a few minutes past ten, and rain fell in a light, steady drizzle; but the sky to the west was ominous, the color of a dusty school blackboard, pregnant with heavy water. I felt cold and irritable. I still had the cough and the constriction in my chest, but I kept trying to convince myself they were psychosomatic; hadn't the damned headache dissolved sometime during the night?

I pulled up the collar on my overcoat and got out and crossed the cobblestones. In the vestibule beyond the arch, a wood-and-glass-paned door let me into a small room with a parqueted wood floor, brightly lighted by ceiling fluorescents; a mellifluous bell above the door announced my entry. Directly across from me was another arch, with maroon curtains swept and tied like portieres at each jamb; beyond, there was another room, identical to the one in which I now stood.

The white-painted walls of both were filled with dozens

of squares and rectangles and oblongs of various dimensions, some alive in vivid color, some brooding darkly—things imitative of Renoir and Monet and Degas; of German impressionists Kirchner, Beckmann, Nolde; of Surrealists such as Dali and Miró. There were also several new ideas and styles that defied categorizing, and no landscapes or seascapes or conventional portraiture. All of it was oil, and all of it original, and all of it—the good, the bad, and the ugly—done by amateurs or unrecognized professionals.

I was looking at a pyrotechnic study in diverse shades of blue, which had both a name and a meaning I did not understand, when a slender, distinguished-looking little man in a neatly trimmed Vandyke beard came through the curtained arch. He wore a dark suit and a multihued tie that might have been painted by one of the artists represented on the gallery walls; his eyes and his carefully brushed hair were the same slate-gray color.

"*Guten Morgen,*" he said, and smiled.

"*Guten Morgen,*" I answered. "Are you Herr Ackermann?"

"Herr Norbert Ackermann, at your service," he said in precise British-accented English. "You are an American?"

"Yes." I introduced myself, and then I said, "A couple of days ago you received a telephone call from a woman named Elaine Kavanaugh—from San Francisco. She asked you about a man named Roy Sands, and about a portrait of him."

The smile chameleoned into a slight frown. "Yes?"

"I represent Miss Kavanaugh," I told him. "I'm investigating the disappearance of her fiancé."

Herr Ackermann's frown deepened. "Surely you cannot think I know anything about this disappearance . . ."

"No, of course not. But Sands did have the name of the Galerie der Expressionisten, and the portrait, as I'm sure Miss Kavanaugh mentioned, was stolen from my apartment. We thought there might be a connection somehow."

"I do not know anyone named Sands. Nor am I aware of

a portrait of the type she described. I made this quite clear to her."

"No one is doubting your word, Herr Ackermann," I said. "But I do have a few additional questions, if you don't mind."

"I suppose not."

"Do you have anyone else working for you, someone who might perhaps have seen or spoken with Sands in some capacity during your absence?"

"I am the sole employee of the Galerie der Expressionisten. In my absence, the front door is locked and no one is admitted."

"Well, do you have any idea why Sands would have been carrying the name and address of your place?"

"Perhaps it was recommended to him by a friend," Herr Ackermann said. "We are quite well known in this area."

"That's a possibility, I guess."

"Your Mr. Sands may have intended to visit the gallery at one time, and did not manage to do so. Or perhaps he did come, and stayed only a short while. There are times when I am busy with other customers."

"Also a possibility," I said. "Tell me, Herr Ackermann, do you handle the work of a large or small number of artists?"

"A fairly large number, I would say. At various times in the past year, at least fifty promising young German artists have been represented in my gallery."

"All impressionists?"

"If you prefer the broad label, yes."

"Do any of them do portraiture?"

"I should suppose some may have at one point or another in their careers attempted portraiture, yes. Do you think one of my artists made this stolen sketch of Mr. Sands?"

"It might explain why he had your gallery's name and address," I said.

"Yes, so it might."

On the chance that Elaine had not mentioned the portrait's bold lines, heavy shadows, and somewhat enlarged, exaggerated masculine features, I related these characteristics to Herr Ackermann. "Do they strike a familiar chord?"

He shook his head. "I'm afraid not. I might possibly be able to recognize the style if I could see the sketch itself—assuming that it was done by someone with whose work I am familiar. However, there are, you must realize, hundreds upon hundreds of would-be or successful artists who may have drawn it, none of whom would be known to me."

I nodded. "Of course."

"I would like to help you," Herr Ackermann said, "but I simply do not know this man Sands; and if he once posed for a sketch done by one of my artists, I have no knowledge of it whatsoever."

I saw no purpose in pressing him further; there was nothing he could or would tell me. I thanked him for his time, politely declined his offer to conduct me through the gallery, and returned to the Volkswagen.

I drove around until I found a *Konditorei* that had a lot of pastry in its front window and a service bar along one wall. I went in and had a cup of coffee and a doughnut with powdered sugar. Afterward I tried my first cigarette of the day, but the coughing began again after three drags; I put it out quickly and brooded into the coffee to keep my mind off my lungs.

It had not been a particularly illuminating trip thus far—and yet, as I had told Elaine, those threatening telephone calls had to mean that there was something important to be found out here. I had hoped that I would learn something further at the Galerie der Expressionisten—a possibility, a direction—but I had apparently been armed with too little information and too much hope. As for the three-day bender MacVeagh had told me about . . . well, there just may have been something in that; it was a puzzling occurrence, in any event.

110

I thought about what Sands had asked Sybille in the Dodge City Bar: *Why did it have to happen?* All right, why did *what* have to happen? Walter the barkeeper had told MacVeagh and me that Sands looked very weary, like an old man, and Sybille had said that he was unhappy. All of which amounted to what?

Saturday, October 30. What had happened on that day that could have put Sands into the kind of low-down blue funk that provokes a guy into a major session with a bottle? Apparently he had been all right when he'd left Larson Barracks to come into Kitzingen that day, so whatever it was likely was not connected with the military installation. Something in Kitzingen, or in the surrounding area, then? That was an angle—not much, maybe, but it was worth looking into.

I returned to the Bayerischer Hof and asked the desk man if there was a daily newspaper circulated in Kitzingen that covered the local news. He told me that the *Main-Post*, which was published in Würzberg to the north, carried all news pertaining to the Main River region. The *Main-Post* had an office in Kitzingen, and he gave me directions to it.

I drove over there, and they had a guy in the small office who spoke English. I told him what I wanted and why, and he put me at an unused desk and disappeared into another room. He came back with a stack of papers covering the week prior to the thirtieth of October, and the Monday and Tuesday following it; after depositing them in front of me, he hovered nearby—either out of curiosity or to make sure that I did not damage any of the editions.

I went through them laboriously, beginning with the paper dated the thirtieth, working backward to the twenty-sixth. I had recalled enough German by now to be able to read most of the headlines and, if anything looked promising, the lead paragraph or two of the accompanying story; when I came to something I could not understand, I asked the guy about it. At the end of an hour, however, I had learned nothing.

I sighed and spread out the issue dated November 1. I went through the initial two pages and half of page three. And I came to the headline spread over three columns at the left-hand margin:

AMERIKANISCHES MÄDCHEN
ERHÄNGT SICH IN KITZINGEN

Translated, that read: AMERICAN GIRL HANGS SELF IN KITZINGEN. I frowned and called the English-speaking guy over and opened my notebook and had him translate the story slowly, so I could write it down as he did so in a form of shorthand I had worked out over the years. It read this way:

Diane Emery, a young American girl and promising artist, hanged herself in her Kitzingen studio at Gartenweg 19 early last Saturday. Suspended from a ceiling fixture by a length of clothesline, her body was discovered by Mrs. Ursula Mende, another tenant of the building.

Miss Emery had lived in Kitzingen for the past year, having studied in Paris for the three years previous. Her oil work has been exhibited in Munich and Paris, as well as locally, and has drawn high praise from critics.

No suicide note was found, and no immediate explanation could be determined for Miss Emery having taken her own life. However, it was conjectured by *Kriminalbeamter* Franz Hüssner that she may have been despondent with personal problems.

That was all—but it was enough to give rise to a small, excited tingling at the base of my neck. This could be the key, the nucleus of the whole affair. Diane Emery had been an artist, a painter, and Roy Sands had sat for a portrait that had some sort of significance; the Emery girl's work had been exhibited locally, and Sands had had the address of the Galerie der Expressionisten. Had they known each other, then? Had knowledge of her death been the reason for Sands' drinking bout? A dozen other questions and half as many suspicions floated across my mind; but I did not as yet have enough information to answer any of them.

I went out to get it.

Herr Ackermann said solemnly, "Ah yes, of course I knew Fräulein Emery. Her death was a terrible tragedy."

"Then she did exhibit some of her paintings here?"

"Yes, several in the past year."

"Was she talented?"

"Oh, very much so," Herr Ackermann said. "She was deeply involved in her work—a true artisan."

"Do you have any idea why she would commit suicide?"

He sighed. "She was also quite an emotional girl, given to many moods, to spells of dark depression. That is the only reply I can offer you."

"The news story hinted at personal problems."

"I know of none in particular," Herr Ackermann said. "I had not seen her for some weeks prior to her death."

"Did she ever confide in you?"

"No. We discussed only art."

"Do you know if she had any special male friends?"

"She spoke of none to me."

"Would you happen to have any of her paintings at the moment?"

"I have two. Following her death, several were purchased." He made a gesture of distaste. "The public can be as swift and as morbid as vultures at times."

"Yeah," I said.

"Would you like to see the paintings?"

"Please."

We went through the curtained arch into the second display room of the gallery. On the far wall, Herr Ackermann indicated a pair of rectangular canvases hung one above the other. I looked closely at them, and they were austere, brooding things painted in dark colors with heavy brush-strokes—and yet both were vivid and compelling. One was called "Deathwatch," and the other "Earthlove": the former depicted, as near as I could tell, a sea of frightened faces staring with Keane-like eyes at a prostrated ancient in a flowing white beard; and the latter grimly portrayed a pair of mounded graves laid side by side, with a man's hand jutting diagonally outward through the spaded earth of one to clasp a woman's hand extended from the other, the third fingers of each encircled by a simple gold wedding band.

A coldness settled on my spine, and I turned away to look at Herr Ackermann. "Was she a fatalist?"

"Perhaps existentialist would be a better term."

"But she *was* preoccupied with death?"

"I suppose you could say she was. Many great artists are, you know."

Ergo, she was fully capable of suicide, I thought. All right, so that proves what? That she killed herself? You knew that from reading the newspaper story. Don't make waves on a calm sea, for Christ's sake.

I studied both paintings again, looking at the style this time rather than the scenes themselves. Even though there seemed to be similarities between these oils and the sketch of Roy Sands—some of the same exaggeration of masculin-ity, for example—I was not enough of a connoisseur to be able to determine beyond a reasonable doubt that she had created the sketch. Maybe Herr Ackermann could have, but as he had said earlier, he would have to have seen the portrait itself in order to make a judgment.

He said, "Do you think Fräulein Emery was acquainted with this man you are seeking—Sands is his name? And that she made this sketch about which you asked me earlier?"

114

"There's a chance of it," I told him. "Did she ever do any portrait work that you know about?"

He shook his head. "She was a true impressionist."

"But she might have—as a favor, or as a gesture of some kind, mightn't she?"

"Perhaps. She was, as I said, an unpredictable girl."

"Okay then. Thanks again for your time, Herr Ackermann."

"I hope you succeed in your quest, sir," he said, and bowed. *"Auf Wiedersehen."*

I walked out and got into the Volkswagen. In my mind's eye I kept seeing that painting called "Earthlove"—the pair of hands reaching out of the graves, clasped together, the wedding rings plainly evident. The morning seemed suddenly colder.

And when I drove away from there, it was with the disturbing mental image of a faceless girl hanging dead and motionless in a room filled with the tools, the wonderment, of creation.

Thirteen

Kriminalbeamter Franz Hüssner was a big, smiling man with heavy blue jowls and bright, quick blue eyes. He wore gray tweed as well as anyone can wear it, and smoked a short white-bowled clay pipe, and had a nervous habit of scratching behind his right ear with the little finger on his right hand. He spoke English in a voice that would have gone well singing *Trink, Trink, Brüderlein, Trink* in a German beer garden, and he was not averse to discussing the Diane Emery suicide with me—especially after he learned my profession. He had never met a private detective, he said, his bright eyes dancing, and to have one from America visit him was indeed an honor. I could not tell if he was putting me on or not.

We sat in his small, spartan office in the Kitzingen *Polizeirevier* and smiled at each other across an old oak desk that was vaguely reminiscent of the one in my own office. Smoke from his clay pipe lay on the air like tule fog in a marsh, and it was aggravating my chest, biting sharply into my lungs with each breath; it smelled as mawkishly sweet as the perfumed joss they burn on Chinese New Year. But Herr Hüssner was on my side now, and I did not want to jeopardize that by insulting his brand of tobacco or his smoking habits; I kept my mouth judiciously shut.

"A sad business, a very sad business," he said at length. "Such a young girl to take her own life. Ach, a terrible thing."

"I understand there was no suicide note," I said.

"That is true."

"She was despondent over personal problems?"

"Yes."

"Any particular personal problems?"

"She was to have a child."

"Oh," I said, "I see."

"A sad business, yes?" He shook his head.

"Were you able to locate the father?"

"No, we were not."

"Then you have no idea who it was?"

"None."

"There was nothing in her personal effects?"

"Fräulein Emery did not keep letters or a journal or photographs."

"And there were no portraits among her paintings?"

"We found only two canvases in her flat—both unfinished and both most definitely not portraits. Her drawing pad contained nothing but blank sheets of paper."

"Uh-huh. Well, what about her friends?"

"She had few friends in Kitzingen," Herr Hüssner said, and went to work behind his ear with the little finger on his right hand. "She was—what do you say?—a lonesome person."

"Yeah."

"Her lover was her private affair, apparently shared with no one."

I studied the backs of my hands. "Were you completely satisfied that her death was suicide?"

Surprisingly, Herr Hüssner smiled. "You suspect murder perhaps?" he asked, as if the idea were gentle insanity.

"No," I said, and gave him an apologetic look. "I was just curious."

"Of course. But no, the death of Fräulein Emery was at her own hands and no others. Frau Mende, who lives in the apartment next door, heard a loud noise from the girl's stu-

118

dio that Saturday and came quickly to investigate. She found the girl still alive and strangling on the clothesline, a chair overturned beneath her. By the time she could summon help, the poor child was dead. A sad, sad business." Herr Hüssner shook his head again and dug behind his ear and raised a great pollutant of gray-blue smoke like a withered wreath about his head.

I said, "Had the Emery girl been known to keep company with military personnel? Or were you able to determine that?"

"We learned little of her private life. You were thinking, perhaps, that the man you are looking for—Herr Sands— was her lover?"

"The idea crossed my mind."

"And why is that?"

I told him, and he nodded thoughtfully. "It is possible you are right. But if so, what would this have to do with Herr Sands' disappearance in America?"

"I don't know yet. I'm still sifting through the haystack."

"What does this mean, sifting through the haystack?"

I explained it to him. He smiled and looked pleased. "The American idiom is wonderful," he said.

"Sure," I agreed. "Was Diane buried here in Kitzingen?"

"No. Her family was notified, from a card we discovered in her purse, and arrangements were made for her to be returned to America by plane."

"I see."

"It was to California," Herr Hüssner said. "You are from San Francisco—that is in California, is it not?"

"Yes," I said. "Where does the Emery girl's family live?"

"The town of Roxbury."

"I don't think I know it."

"It is near—what is it?—ah yes, Eureka. We wished to cable the family of the tragedy and it was necessary to send the cable to this Eureka."

The air in there was cloying now, and very hot, and I

wanted nothing so much than to get up and open the window behind Herr Hüssner's desk; I could see the cold, fresh rain beading and running on the glass outside. I forced myself to sit still, and said, "Would you mind telling me the address, Herr Hüssner?"

"Do you plan to see the Emerys when you are again in America?"

"Well, possibly. I'm not sure just yet."

"Of course," he said, and smiled knowingly, and got up on his feet. "A moment, please?"

"Sure."

He went out and shut the door, and I stared hungrily at the rain on the window glass. I coughed into my handkerchief and tried not to dwell on implications just yet, not with the atmosphere the way it was. Two or three minutes went by, and Herr Hüssner came back with a folder and sat down behind his desk again.

He spread the folder open and moved a sheaf of papers aside. On top of them was a photograph. I tried to look at it upside down and gave that idea up almost immediately. I said, "Is that a picture of Diane Emery?"

"Yes."

"May I see it?"

"If you wish."

He handed it to me, and it was a death-scene shot, a close-up of the girl's body after they had cut her down from where she had hanged herself. Mercifully, someone had closed her mouth and her eyelids, and you could not see the marks the clothesline must have left on her throat. Her features were contorted, swollen, but the intrinsic beauty which had been hers was apparent; she had been slim, dark, long-featured, with hair cropped close to her head. She looked very young—very young.

I put the photograph back on the sheaf of papers, face down. "How old was she?" I asked quietly.

"Twenty-four."

120

"Nobody should die at twenty-four," I said. "Twenty-four is an age for living, an age for laughing."

Herr Hüssner glanced up at me, and now his smile was gentle and sad. "Life can be very cruel at times," he said.

"Yeah."

Silence settled for a long moment, and then I looked at Herr Hüssner and I knew that he was thinking the same things I was—two middle-aged cops looking back on all the injustices and all the cruelties which had been wreaked on man by man in two worlds not so different, not so far apart. What happened in Germany thirty-five years ago could have happened in America, could still happen in America, because man was the most callous of beings, the rational beast, the thinking predator, destroying himself and his species and never knowing—this superior, intelligent creature—the *why* of it, of any of it . . .

Herr Hüssner shuffled papers and sighed and said, "The girl's parents are Mr. and Mrs. Daniel Emery, twenty-six nineteen Coachman Road, Roxbury, California."

I wrote that down in my notebook, closed it, and got on my feet. I had no more business here, and as much as I enjoyed Herr Hüssner's company, I needed to get out of that room very quickly. I said, "I appreciate all the help you've given me, Herr Hüssner."

"*Keine Ursache,*" he answered graciously.

"If I find out anything that might interest you on this matter, I'll let you know."

"That would be very kind."

"*Auf Wiedersehen,* Herr Hüssner."

"*Alles Gute, meine Freunde.*"

The cold sweetness of the rain outside was like an oxygen resuscitator to a man dying of cyanide-gas poisoning . . .

At the Bayerischer Hof, I asked the desk man to confirm a reservation for me on the earliest flight from Frankfurt to

London the next day, and to get me onto the first polar flight to San Francisco following my arrival at Heathrow. Then I wrote out a brief telegram to Elaine Kavanaugh, telling her I was leaving Germany and that I would come to see her as soon as I arrived back in San Francisco. That would have to do in place of my promised telephone call.

It could be, I knew, that my decision to leave was premature, but I had to make a choice and my instincts had called for this one from the moment I had left Herr Hüssner's office. I could spend another couple of days in Kitzingen, but it seemed pointless in view of what I had learned—the implications, the direction, of what I had learned. I fully intended to use the remainder of this day in trying to uncover further information on Sands, on the portrait; I had the feeling, however, that I had already found out most, if not all, of what there was to be found in Germany.

I went up to my room and sat drinking hot coffee, letting my mind work over what I now had. I got it into an orderly progression after a time, and it went like this:

Roy Sands is not so much different from his circle of friends as it had first appeared; like MacVeagh and the others, he is an aging lover, a cocksman who needs the reassurance of his desirability and his manhood—and even though he's in love with Elaine Kavanaugh, and plans to marry her, he happens to be in Germany and she happens to be in the States. A hard-on having no conscience, as they say, he goes prowling and he meets pretty, young, emotional Diane Emery. They have a thing—maybe casual for both in the beginning, maybe immediately deeper than a shallow physical relationship for the girl.

For one reason or another—Sands' reticent nature is such that his ego does not require the verbal feeding of one such as MacVeagh's, or he is afraid of word leaking back to Elaine —he keeps his affair with Diane strictly to himself. But in a weak moment he allows her to make a sketch of him, which she then presents to him as a token of her love or esteem or whatever. He ~~cannot bring~~ himself ~~to destroy~~ the sketch, and so he puts it in with the things he is shipping back to Elaine, knowing that under normal circumstances she won't pry.

Aside from the sketch, Sands is very careful. He meets Diane only in Kitzingen, perhaps at her apartment, perhaps at a café or restaurant—and perhaps at the Galerie der Expressionisten. She frequents the establishment, since her paintings are on exhibit there, and so on some occasion she gives him the name and address and he writes it down and if he rendezvous with her there, it is outside somewhere; Herr Ackermann never sees him.

The affair progresses, with dozens of possible nuances unexplainable just now—and then the girl becomes pregnant. Sands' interest in her has apparently been little more than the scratching of an itch, but it has become far more than that for Diane; she's fallen in love with him. Maybe she asks him to marry her, but even if he wanted to do the right thing by her, he is unable to; he's in love with Elaine, and the choice between the two of them is no contest. He tells Diane that he can't marry her, perhaps offering to pay for an adoption or an abortion.

But the girl does not take his rejection of her love and her love-child in the worldly manner in which he expects. She is an earthlover, hands clasped to and from the grave, and life on any other terms is unthinkable for her; the rejection is absolute. So on one fine Saturday she makes her decision and she ties a length of clothesline around a light fixture and around her throat and destroys herself and her baby in a single strangling, suspended *danse macabre*.

Sands, on that same day, has some kind of appointment with the girl and he goes to her studio; there he discovers what has happened—one of the neighbors tells him, maybe, or he sees the *Polizei* removing her body. He is horrified, shocked, grieved; whatever else Sands may be, he is also a man with feelings, with a conscience. He blames himself for the girl's death, and the guilt is too much for him to bear. He goes to the cheapest *Kneipe* in the city—the Dodge City Bar—and he asks Sybille, "Why did it have to happen?", and then he drinks himself into a three-day stupor.

When MacVeagh locates him on the following Monday, and sobers him up, Sands has lost some of the deep, unbearable guilt. He *still feels* responsible for what happened, but it is done and finished now, and torturing himself will not bring Diane back. So he comes out of it, more reticent than ever, and until he is returned to the States for discharge he stays close to home, filling his days and his nights with visions of Elaine . . .

Well, I thought, okay. It all fits, and that's fine. But there are still too many unanswered questions. Like: How does all of this fit in with Sands' disappearance? And why is that portrait important to the person in San Francisco who made those threatening telephone calls to Elaine and me? And why does that person want Sands' affair with Diane Emery to remain a buried secret—if, in fact, that was the reason or part of the reason he tried to keep me out of Germany?

Since the entire episode with Diane Emery—assuming, of course, that the connection between the two existed in reality and not only inside my head—took place in Germany, there conceivably could be no connection between the vanishing of Sands and the affair. If it were not for that portrait and its as yet unexplained importance, which made for a strong link between the two. And if it were not for one other nagging little fact that formed a nebulous but potentially important connection.

Diane Emery's parents lived in Roxbury, California, near the city of Eureka—and Eureka was in the northern part of the state, approximately halfway between San Francisco and Eugene, Oregon, the two places where Sands had last been seen.

I got out of my chair and paced awhile, remembering what Chuck Hendryx had told me about his brief meeting

124

with Sands at the Presidio in San Francisco. Well, suppose the something Sands had said he had to do before meeting Elaine was to see the parents of the girl whose death he had indirectly caused—either because the guilt was still strong in him and confession was a balm for an aching soul, or for some other intangible reason. If so, *had* he gone to Roxbury? Or had something detoured him to Eugene first? And if he had stopped in Roxbury, was the key to his eventual disappearance to be found there?

I stopped pacing and sat down again, and the telephone bell sounded. It was the desk man to tell me that there was a flight leaving Frankfurt at eight-thirty in the morning, and a polar non-stop departing London at one tomorrow afternoon; I was confirmed on both flights. I thanked him and put the receiver down and got my suitcase out of the closet.

After I had packed, I went downstairs and out into the rain again, to see if there was anything more to be unearthed. When I came back six hours later—having spoken to Diane Emery's neighbors, to a couple of casual acquaintances of Roy Sands at Larson Barracks, to the proprietor of another, smaller art gallery—I had the answer to that: there was nothing.

I told myself once more that I was making the right decision in leaving, picked up my suitcase and my car from the Bayerischer Hof, and began the trip back to Frankfurt and home.

Fourteen

I came back to San Francisco the same way I had arrived in Germany: bone-tired.

There had been delays at Heathrow again, and inclement weather on the transatlantic flight, and it was after three when the plane landed at San Francisco International on Wednesday. I had regained the nine hours lost going over, and so it was midnight European time and better than eighteen hours since I had last slept.

It was cold and clear in The City, and that was a pleasant change from the sweeping rain and snow which had blanketed most of Europe. I took the shuttle into the Downtown Terminal, went directly from there to the Argonaut Hotel.

Not quite as genteel as the Royal Gate, it was nonetheless another of those gilt-edged mirrors of old San Francisco; Elaine Kavanaugh had, for one thing, excellent taste. I spoke to a desk clerk who might have been a younger brother of the one at the Royal Gate, found out that Elaine was in her room, and waited while he had me announced. A couple of minutes later he came back with her approval and told me I would find her in 722.

When I came out of the elevator on the seventh floor, she had her door open at the far end of the hall, waiting for me. She wore a yellow sweater and a plaid skirt, and her hair was carelessly combed, her face haggard and etched with desperate hope and infinite weariness. There were purplish half-moons under her eyes, and worry lines on her forehead and at the corners of her unpainted mouth. Her flesh had a loose quality, a kind of mass relaxation of the molecules of her being, and she looked at least as old as I am.

If I tell her what I suspect, I thought, she'll age even more, she'll disintegrate right here in front of me. The prospect was an ugly one. During the plane flights I had tried to think of different ways of handling my meeting with her, using half-truths at this or that level, but none of it was particularly appealing. Finally, I had decided to just let it happen spontaneously, *que será será,* and that still seemed to be the best idea.

She caught my arm and drew me inside, and then shut the door and leaned back against it, looking at me with those desperate eyes. "My God, I thought you were never going to come," she said. "I've been waiting and waiting—why didn't you *say* something in your wire?"

"There was nothing immediate to say."

"But didn't you find out something?"

"I don't know yet."

"What does that mean? Did you or didn't you?"

"I'm just not sure."

"There must be *some* reason you decided to come home so quickly, for God's sake."

"There's a possibility I have to check out," I said. "Some people your fiancé may have gone to see in Northern California."

"Where in Northern California?"

"A town called Roxbury."

"Where's that? I've never heard of it."

"It's near Eureka."

"Who would Roy know up there?"

"The family of someone he . . . met over in Germany."

"Why would he go to visit this family?"

"I didn't say that he did."

"But you think he might have?"

128

"There's the chance."

"But why? Why would he do that before coming to me?"

"I'm . . . not sure."

"Who was this someone he met in Germany?"

"Just a guy," I lied automatically, and I felt uncomfortable, I felt lousy about this whole damned thing. I could not look at Elaine. I went to the window across the room and stared out at the city, lighting a cigarette; my cough had gone away again, the way it always did, and I knew I was back fighting to keep myself under a pack a day, same old circus, same old carousel.

She came up behind me, and I could see her reflection in the window glass. I said, "Have you been all right?"

"I'm beginning to understand what people with claustrophobia must feel like."

"But you didn't go out."

"No. And no one has bothered me."

"Well, I'm glad to hear that."

"Look at me," she said, and there was some of that desperation in her voice now.

I did not want to look at her, but I turned anyway, slowly, and met her eyes and tried to keep my own blank and gentle. She said, "Why won't you tell me what you found out? About these people Roy might have gone to see?"

"Because I'm not sure it means anything. I don't want to get your hopes up."

"I have a right to know. You're working for *me*, you know."

"Listen, Miss Kavanaugh, bear with me a little. I'm not withholding anything important. I just want to have a chance to look into this thing before I talk about it. That's all."

"Does it have something to do with that portrait of Roy?"

"It might."

"Did you find out anything about it in Germany?"

"Possibly."

"What?"

"I don't want to talk about it just yet."

"Do you have an idea now why it's important?"

"No," I said truthfully.

"Or who stole it? Or who made those telephone calls?"

"No."

"Or where Roy is now?"

"No."

Her eyes searched my face, the pupils moving, fluttering like restless birds. Finally she pivoted and crossed the room and sank into one of the chairs. She sat with her hands twisted together in an attitude of prayer, staring down at them, not moving. Then, abruptly, her head snapped up and she said, "He's dead, isn't he?"

"What?"

"That's why you won't tell me what you learned in Germany. You think he's dead, for some reason you think he's dead, and you want to make sure before you tell me. That's it, isn't it?"

"No," I said, "no, that's not it."

She caught her lower lip between her teeth and bit at it until I thought she might draw blood. Her eyes were on her hands again. Silence gathered thickly in the room, and I watched her and tried to think of something to say that wouldn't sound false and unconvincing—but there seemed to be nothing. I felt like a damned heel, and yet there was no other way to do it without being even more cruel; I had only suspicions, not facts.

She broke the silence after a long moment, and her voice was flat, empty, teetering on the edge of hysteria. "Yes, he's dead, I know he's dead and you know it too, that has to be it."

"Miss Kavanaugh, please—"

"He's dead, he died somehow and I'll never see him again—oh God, oh God, he's dead, damn you, I know he's dead, why don't you tell me, I know *he's dead!*" She began to rock back and forth like a little girl with a doll in her lap, clutching her hands, her mouth quivering.

I went to her, awkwardly, hurriedly, and took her shoulders. "Easy now, it's all right," I said, and the words were banal in my own ears. "You don't know he's dead, I don't know it, I don't even think it—"

"No, he's dead," she said, "he's the only man I ever loved, the only man I was ever with, we were lovers, listen, we were lovers and I don't care because we *loved*, we loved, it was beautiful every time, oh my God, I wish I was dead too . . ."

Her eyes were fixed, catatonic, and bubbles of saliva formed at the corners of her mouth. I slapped her, hard enough to jerk her head around, reddening her cheek. Her mouth went slack, and then her eyes cleared and she blinked at me, focused on me, and the dangerous moment—the potentially suicidal moment—was over. She was all right again, embarrassed, and she put her face in her hands and began to cry, softly, quietly.

I left her and returned to the window, looking out at the city again, at the inanimate testimonials of civilization and all its subtle barbarity. After a time the muffled sobbing sounds ceased behind me, and Elaine said, "I'm sorry, I . . . I didn't mean to act that way."

"You don't have to apologize," I said without turning.

"I don't usually lose control of myself like that . . ."

I faced her then. The crying had been good for her, a kind of catharsis; there was more animation in her face now, color in her cheeks, life in her eyes. "You've been under a heavy strain, Miss Kavanaugh."

"Yes," she said. "Yes."

"In all honesty, I don't know or even think that your fiancé is dead. What I found out in Germany may not even have anything to do with his disappearance. It's just something that I want to look into a little further, and after I have, then I'll tell you about it. I know it's rough, but I'm asking you to do this my way; and I promise you that the minute I find out something definite on his whereabouts, I'll let you know."

She nodded convulsively. "All right," she said. "I . . . I trust you."

I felt even more like a heel. I got another cigarette into my mouth and said, "I'll be leaving for Roxbury first thing tomorrow morning. Do you think you can stand it here another day or two?"

"Yes."

"Are you sure?"

"Yes. I'll be fine." She looked away from me. "What I said about Roy and me, well, I mean . . ."

"If I heard anything," I told her, "I've already forgotten what it was."

"Thank you."

I suggested, pointlessly, that she try to relax, and said that I would call her from Roxbury sometime the next day. Then I touched her shoulder, lightly, and left her alone again . . .

I picked up my car at the parking garage across from the Downtown Terminal, and it was almost five-thirty when I drove out into the heavy rush-hour traffic which clogs downtown San Francisco between four and six on weekday afternoons. I thought briefly about going home for a shower and a change of clothes, decided I did not really feel much like looking at the emptiness of my flat, and found myself on Geary Boulevard, heading west toward the ocean.

Saxon's 19th Avenue Coffee Shop was out that way, on the other side of the Park.

I had not had much time to think about Cheryl the past couple of days, but she had been there in a corner of my mind nonetheless. I wanted to see her tonight, I wanted to talk to her. I had no idea if she was working the day or the night shift; but even with the traffic, I knew I could get to

19th Avenue by six o'clock and that way meet her either coming or going.

I preferred seeing her at Saxon's to calling or stopping by her home for the simple reason that I did not want to talk to her brother. He was a suspect in the theft of the portrait of Roy Sands, the threatening telephone calls, just as Chuck Hendryx and Rich Gilmartin were suspects. I was also not forgetting about Nick Jackson, even though there did not seem to be any way Jackson could have known that I had the sketch, that I was going to Germany at the behest of Elaine Kavanaugh. The truth was, I had had difficulty envisioning Rosmond as the one responsible—simply because he was Cheryl's brother; and yet I still did not want to talk to him on this day. If he and Hendryx and Gilmartin thought I was still in Germany, I would feel better about things; it seemed important that I make the trip to Roxbury without any of them knowing I had even returned to the country.

When I reached Saxon's, it was five before six. I parked around the first corner beyond the coffee shop, illegally, and walked back through a cold, light fog—and Cheryl was just coming out of the front door. She came to a complete standstill when she saw me, and then a small, faintly shy smile gently curved the corners of her mouth.

"Hi," I said.

"Hi."

"Day shift today?"

She nodded, and her fingers were nervous at the buttons of the dark beige coat she wore. Under it was a simple beige wool jersey—she had obviously changed out of whatever uniform she was required to wear at Saxon's—and her autumn-hued hair was tied with a bright turquoise ribbon well below the neck, so that the soft reddish-gold was like a fan behind her head and like a proud and sleekly curried tail extending down her back. She looked very lovely.

"When did you get home from Germany?" she asked.

"This afternoon."

"Did you learn anything more about Roy?"

"Not much," I said. "Nothing definite." I looked into her eyes, kept on looking into them; they said a lot of things, some of the same things mine were saying to her. "I hope you don't mind my coming out here like this, but I wanted to see you tonight, if only for just a few minutes. I left downtown at five-thirty, and it seemed easier to just drive out here rather than wait until later to call."

"No," she said, "I don't mind. I'm glad you did."

I wanted to touch her; instead I kept my hands firmly in the pockets of my coat. "Were you going any place special now? Or just home?"

"Home."

"Would you like to have a drink with me? And then dinner? I know it's kind of short notice, and if you're busy tonight I'll understand."

"I'm not busy," Cheryl said. "I hadn't planned on anything at all this evening. Doug had to go to the Presidio for something today and he probably won't be back until very late."

There was a pleasant warmth in the core of my stomach. "Shall we go now?"

"Do you think I ought to change first?"

"You look fine, Cheryl. You look wonderful."

We went to the Cossack, on Clement, and had two cocktails in the lounge and then dinner in one of the private booths in the restaurant section: chicken Kiev and sour red cabbage and demitasse cups of bitter Turkish coffee afterward. It was dark and quiet in there. The waiters wore Russian Cossack uniforms replete with scimitars, and hidden speakers gave out with Mussorgsky and Shostakovich and some of the other Russian composers at low volume.

It was fine between us, easy and warm. When I touched her hand with the tips of my fingers once during dinner, she did not stiffen and her eyes reflected in the glow of the candlelight a growing trust and a growing need that was exciting and touching and very real.

134

We talked about many things, impersonal and personal, jumping from this to that as each of us sought to explore the other's depths, the interests and prejudices and likes and dislikes that each of us had, seeking the common bonds and dwelling on them when we found them. She laughed when I told her about my collection of pulp magazines, and the tenacity with which I had pursued the hobby, but it was not a mocking laugh or a censorious one—as Erika's had been; it was a pleased, curious laugh, as if she were fascinated by the idea of anyone indulging in that sort of hobby. And then she wanted to know if I thought the idea of a grown woman collecting dolls from foreign lands was silly. No, I didn't think that was silly at all. Well, she said, she had sixteen dolls in her bedroom, from such countries as Spain and Holland and France and England and Mexico and Germany and Japan, maybe she would show them to me one day if I was interested. Yes, I was interested, and did she want to see some of my pulp magazines?—making a small joke about their being the lure to my apartment instead of etchings. She laughed softly and we went on to something else without any pauses or awkwardness.

We discovered that we both liked hiking in the woods, old movies—Charlie Chan and *The Falcon* and Bogart and Peter Lorre and Lloyd Nolan—brandy old-fashioneds, football, and good soul jazz. We disliked parking meters, junk mail, the drug culture, peanut butter, and the travesties of war. We touched on religion and politics just long enough to determine that our ideas were similar on one and dissimilar on the other.

We talked and we talked, open and natural, like old friends, like new lovers, and I forgot for a little while about Roy Sands and poor Elaine Kavanaugh and all the ugliness and suspected ugliness that had touched my life in the past week. All at once, then, it was midnight and they were about to close up. We asked each other where the time had gone, the way you do, and I paid the check and then I drove her directly back to 19th Avenue, parking in front of her car a half-block from Saxon's.

We sat there on the darkened street. I said, because it had to be said, "Cheryl, will you do me a favor?"

"Yes, if I can."

"Don't mention that you saw me tonight. To your brother, or to anyone."

"Why?"

"My reasons are complicated and not exactly explainable just now. I'll tell you about them a little later. Okay?"

"Well . . . of course, if it's what you want."

"Thanks, honey."

She turned her face close to mine at the endearment, and her eyes were pools of deep blackness with the faintest traces of light deep at their centers—and I kissed her. She did not pull away and her lips parted slightly under mine, warm and soft and sweet, and I could feel her shudder with inner emotion as I held her shoulders lightly in my hands. I drew back finally, looking at her, wanting her, needing her, sensing the same feelings inside her own body, but this was not the time, the time was perhaps soon and we both knew that, I think, we both were unable to deny that, but it was not just yet.

"Thank you," she said in a soft, liquid whisper, "thank you for a lovely evening."

"Are you working Saturday night?"

"No—the day shift."

"Can I see you then? I have to go away again, but I should be back by Saturday."

"Yes," she said.

She touched my hand and we said good night, and then she was out of the car and walking quickly to her own. I sat watching her until she had driven off, until her taillights had vanished around the corner on 19th Avenue, before starting my own car.

The taste and the touch and the scent of her stayed with me all the way back to my apartment.

136

Fifteen

Roxbury was a small town like a thousand, five thousand other small towns spread across the United States—a little more rustic, perhaps, because of its location, but otherwise predictably conventional. It was situated in the thickly wooded foothills of the Klamath Mountains, east and a little south of Eureka; there was a single street bisecting it into equal halves and extending for three blocks, and that was called Main Street and had everything on it that you would expect to find on Main Street, U.S.A. The village looked quiet and sleepy, and the towering giants of the Redwood Empire, which ringed it majestically, gave it an atmosphere of bucolic tranquillity.

I got in there a few minutes past two on Friday afternoon, and it was cool and cloudy, the countryside lushly green and water-jeweled from a recent rain. I had been on the road for something like six hours, including a brief stop in Ukiah for lunch, and I was tired and cramped as I drove along Main Street. The car had not overheated on the drive, but a rattling sound had developed somewhere, in a location I could not pinpoint. It failed to surprise me much.

At the far edge of town, I found a motel called the Redwood Lodge. It had eight cabins set into a rough horseshoe shape, with number one and number eight at the points of the shoe; they were spaced far apart and partially hidden from one another by redwoods and heavy forest growth. In the near-center of the shoe was a large office-and-residence, of the same design as the cabins and fronted with a jungle of ferns.

I stopped in, and a guy who looked a little like Frank Lovejoy rented me number five for eight dollars a night; I was his first customer all week, he said, things were pretty slow this time of year, big rain and all keeps the people away from the scenic areas. He took me out to the cabin personally; it was two rooms and a shower bath, with beamed ceilings and a false fireplace and mountain-cabin furnishings. I asked the guy how you got to Coachman Road, and he told me and wished me a pleasant stay and left me to my own devices.

I changed into a pair of slacks and a light jacket, and got back into the car and continued east and found Coachman Road without difficulty. It was a narrow, humped lane winding upward through heavy copse of redwood and pine, paralleling a small stream swollen by the winter rains. I went about a mile, and a post mailbox appeared to the left; you could just make out the numerals 2619 on the side of it. Beyond the box, an open gate gave on a sideless wooden platform spanning the creek. On the opposite bank a clearing had been cut in the trees and there was a white frame house on it, and a small barn, and a bare front yard containing a Dodge pickup half as old as I was and the bones of a couple of mid-Depression Fords. The hood on the pickup was raised, and a big guy dressed in blue coveralls had his head inside the engine compartment. He pulled it out when the loose boards of the platform protested the weight of my car, and watched me drive up and park to one side of where he was.

I got out and went over to the Dodge. There was an old, battered toolbox open on the ground by the front fender, and beside it, on a piece of grease-marked canvas, were the components of a two-barrel carburetor. The cool, crisp air smelled of conifers and damp vegetation and oil and machinery corrosion.

The guy was about forty, and he had a face like a rubber

138

mask—or a dead man. The lips were thick and bluish-red, the skin had the look and consistency of dried tallow, the eyes were black pouched pits filled with vacuousness. He had thick, muscle-bunched shoulders and hands like the jaws of a scoop shovel. He was watching me curiously, neither friendly nor unfriendly, those empty, bottomless eyes as immobile as a snake's.

I put a smile on for him. "Hi," I said.

"Howdy," ponderously, atonally.

"Is this the Emery place?"

"Yeah."

"Are you Mr. Emery? Daniel Emery?"

"No, Mr. Emery he went into Eureka today."

"Oh, I see."

"My name's Holly. I work for Mr. Emery."

"Well, I'm glad to meet you, Holly."

"Mrs. Emery, she's up at the house if you want to see her."

"I'll do that, thanks."

"Sure," Holly said.

He turned, dismissing me, and got his head inside the engine compartment of the pickup again. I watched him working in there with a box-head wrench for a moment, and then I moved away and went toward the white frame house.

It was a shambling old structure with dull green shutters and a peaked roof and starched chintz curtains in the windows. There was a vegetable garden along one side, and some thin-vined climbing roses clinging like ivy to a trellis built against the right front wall. As I approached, the front door opened and a woman stepped out a few paces, staring at me.

She was very thin, very gaunt, with gray hair that seemed to grow in tufts on a sunken, colorless skull. A crooked witchlike nose protruded from the center of an angular face; above it were two small, lashless eyes with all the color long since faded out of them, and below were blood-

139

less, almost nonexistent lips. Her calves and ankles, visible beneath the hem of an old-fashioned black skirt, were like white birch poles interwoven with the ugly blue threading of varicose veins. She wore an old gray sweater buttoned to her throat, and white ankle socks and dusty nurse-fashion oxfords, and she had about her a look of infinite weariness, infinite hardship—the way the pioneer women of the mid-1800's must have looked after twenty or thirty years of plains life.

She said, "Yes? Was there something?" She had a shrill, querulous voice, like the cry of a frightened crow.

"Mrs. Emery?"

"That's right. What is it?"

"I'd like a few words with you, if I may."

"About what?"

"About your daughter—Diane."

Her head jerked slightly, and her eyes seemed to lift in their sockets, darting, and again I was reminded of a frightened crow. She reached up with her right hand and gathered the material of her sweater tightly at her throat. "My daughter's dead. She died, over in Germany, three months ago."

"Yes," I said gently, "I know."

"I don't have none of her paintings. She never give us none of her paintings, if that's what you want."

"No, that isn't what I want."

"Some people come around here, wanted her paintings, but we never had none of them." There was a faintly bitter note in her voice, as if the fact that Diane had not given her mother and father any of her valuable art was as much of an injustice and as much of a tragedy as the girl's death.

"I'm not here about any paintings, Mrs. Emery," I said.

"What is it, then?"

"Do you know a man named Roy Sands?"

She did that lifting, darting thing with her eyes again, and her mouth disappeared completely in an ugly white slash, like a razor cut just before it starts to bleed. "That

140

filth," she said shrilly. "He killed her, he killed my Diane girl."

I stared at her. "What?"

"He got her in the family way, and she destroyed herself on account of him, God have mercy. Him, that Army man, that filth."

"You're certain he was the father of your daughter's child?"

"He said it, he come here and he said he was—coming around here, trying to say he was sorry."

"When, Mrs. Emery? When was he here?"

"Just before Christmas, come spoiling Christmas, come just when Dan and Holly was putting up the little tree. He come and took coffee with us, saying he knew her, he knew our Diane, and then he told us he was the father of her baby and he was sorry, he was *sorry* they was both dead!"

"Do you remember what day it was that he was here?"

"Just before Christmas."

"Yes, but what *day?*"

"Monday, day after church."

"You're sure of that?"

Mrs. Emery looked at me, blinking, eyes darting. "Listen, who are you, mister? What're you asking questions about him, that Sands, for?"

"I'm trying to find him," I said. "He's disappeared."

"Disappeared?"

"Yes, apparently soon after he was here."

"You a friend of his, mister?"

"No, I've been—"

"What you want here, mister?"

"I told you, Mrs. Emery, I'm trying to find Roy Sands."

"I don't know where he is, I don't ever want to know where he is, that Army filth. We sent him packing, and he went, too, with his tail down like the dog he is— You listen here, I hope you never find him, I hope the good Lord put him down in hell for what he done to my little girl."

"Mrs. Emery—"

"No, now you get out of here, I don't want you here."

"Please, it's important that I—"

"Get out of here!" she shouted. "You get out of here!"

She backed away, still clutching the sweater at her throat, a kind of wildness in her faded eyes now. I stood looking at her, indecisive; then I heard pounding steps behind me and Holly was there, the rubber mask pinched and tight and the vacuous pits radiating molten light in their depths.

"What'd you do?" he said. "What'd you do to Mrs. Emery?"

"Nothing," I said. "I didn't do anything to her."

"Get out of here!" the woman screamed at me. "Get out of here, go away, you, don't you come back!"

"You better do what she says, mister," Holly said softly, but his big hands hooked and curled at his waist and I knew that if I tried to linger, to reason with Mrs. Emery, he would jump me. Things could be very bad then, in a lot of ways. It was her property, after all.

I raised my hands, palms outward. "All right," I said. "I'm going."

"Go on, then," Holly said.

I backed off a couple of steps and turned with the hairs on the nape of my neck prickling. But he did not move from beside her. I walked away, slowly, and got into my car. I looked up at them, then, and they were still standing by the door to the white frame house, both of them looking down at me, this Holly with his jawlike hands still curled and Mrs. Emery still clutching her sweater at her throat.

I swung the car around and went over the platform, thinking: Poor Diane, poor genius. Maybe I can understand why death for you was preferable to coming home . . .

Sixteen

So all right.

My suspicions were confirmed, and it did not make me feel very good that they had been. I hoped that I would not have to tell Elaine Kavanaugh—trusting, loving Elaine Kavanaugh—that her fiancé had been the father of Diane Emery's child in Kitzingen, Germany, and that it was apparently because of him she had committed suicide by hanging. If I could locate him, I knew I would say nothing to her; what point was there in releasing skeletons, in destroying individually created sainthood, if you could preserve happiness and a kind of love that had a shaky but potentially supportive foundation? Well, I *had* to find Sands, that was the simple fact of it. The prospect of having to tell Elaine what I knew, of having her drag it out of me as she would surely do, was painfully depressing. It was bad enough to be poking into other people's lives, but when you had to air their dirty linen in front of them, as the old saying goes, it reaffirmed the grim comment Eberhardt had once made to me when I was still on the force: of all the grim messengers on this earth, a cop is the grimmest—a kind of Fifth Horseman of the Apocalypse carrying news of death and tragedy and terror into the homes of those who pay his salary . . .

I got my mind off that track—some track—and back onto what I now knew of the activities of Roy Sands. He had definitely come here to Roxbury after leaving San Francisco

143

on the nineteenth of last month; and on the twentieth he had visited the Emery farm, presumably for the purpose I had conjectured in Kitzingen: a lingering guilt at having been responsible for Diane's death, and a slim hope that confession to her parents would give succor to his disturbed soul. But the Emerys had driven him away, offering him no forgiveness, no understanding.

And then?

Well, he had apparently left Roxbury, by one means of transportation or another, and gone directly to Eugene, Oregon, for some as yet unexplained reason. Had he done that the same day he visited the Emerys—Monday? It would not appear so, since he had checked into the Eugene hotel late on the twenty-first, Tuesday, and had sent the wires to Hendryx, Rosmond, and Gilmartin on that same evening.

After that—blank.

If Sands had spent the night of the twentieth here, he would not have had much choice of location; aside from the Redwood Lodge, where I was now staying, I had noticed a small hotel on Main Street and nothing else—although there may have been some kind of accommodations on one of the side streets. I ought to be able, then, to determine, with no problem, whether or not he had spent that particular evening in Roxbury. After that, I would just have to see what developed, what my instincts told me. I had this feeling, a prescience of sorts, that said the answer to the disappearance of Roy Sands was in this village—that the final solution to the whole affair could be had right here, with just a little digging, a little perseverance. There was no foundation for that feeling, and yet it was there and it was demanding.

I drove back to the Redwood Lodge and stopped at the office and talked again to the guy who looked like Frank Lovejoy. His name was Jardine, I discovered, and he was the owner of the motel; when I told him what my job was and asked him about Roy Sands, he was agreeably cooperative.

144

"Sure," he said, "I remember him clear enough—Roy Sands. He came in on foot, with just a single suitcase. It was raining a little that day, and he came shuffling down the road looking kind of wet and forlorn. Must have just got off the one o'clock bus from Eureka, I remember thinking at the time. Let's see, I rented him cabin number three, I think it was. Only stayed the one night."

"He was alone?"

"Oh sure, alone."

"Did he say much to you?"

"Come to think of it, he asked me for Coachman Road. Same as you did a while ago."

"Anything else?"

"Not as I can remember."

"What time did he leave the next morning?"

"I couldn't say," Jardine answered. "He was gone, key in the cabin door, when Frances—that's my old lady—went in at ten."

"Then you didn't see him leave?"

"No."

"Isn't it a little unusual for somebody to check out that way, without turning the key in to you here?"

"Not if they've paid in advance, like he did."

"Okay," I said. "Can you tell me where the bus station is?"

"Don't have one, exactly. Greyhounds stop at Vanner's Emporium, two blocks back on Main."

"Is there a police station in Roxbury?"

"Well, yeah."

"Where would I find it?"

"In the City Hall. Same block as Vanner's Emporium, one street north. State Street."

"Thanks."

"Sure," Jardine said. "Glad to oblige."

I went to Vanner's Emporium first, and a very old man with the look and actions of a centenarian told me that he didn't remember selling a ticket to anybody who looked like Roy Sands, but maybe he had, since his memory wasn't so good here the past couple of years. He also told me that there were buses to Eureka every other day—Monday, Wednesday, Friday, at 2:00 P.M. You could make connections there for Eugene. Buses south or east? Tuesdays, Thursdays, Saturdays, and Sundays to Redding, departing 1:00 P.M.

I walked down the block a couple of doors to a café and had some coffee and watched nightfall enfolding the ancient, monolithic redwoods. Apparently Sands had not gone to Eugene by bus; he had spent the night of Monday, the twentieth, in Roxbury, and there were no Greyhounds out to Eureka and eventually Eugene on Tuesday. He could not have gone to Redding on the 1:00 P.M. Monday bus; that was the one he had come in on, according to what Jardine at the Redwood Lodge had told me. So even if there were some explanation for his heading south to Redding instead of west to Eureka for the transfer to Eugene, he could not have gotten by bus to Redding to do it. Still, he had been in Eugene on Tuesday night, the twenty-first, to send wires and to check into the Leavitt Hotel; he had to have gotten there somehow.

Had he left Roxbury by train, then? I had not seen anything remotely resembling a railroad depot, and I doubted seriously that a town as small as this one would have passenger service. Sands had not had a car, that had been confirmed by Jardine. Taxi? Possible. But even if Roxbury had some type of cab service, and I suspected that they did not, the cost seemed prohibitive. That left hitchhiking and/or a private vehicle of some kind.

I thought again of Nick Jackson. Was it possible that Jackson, who had been touring the Northwest with this WAC nurse, had drifted into California as far south as Roxbury—and that Sands had met him here, gone with him to Eugene for some reason? Possible, yes, but not probable; the coincidence of a chance meeting like that was a little too

146

much to swallow. The more I thought about things, the more I was inclined to eliminate Jackson—he seemed too far removed from the core of the whole affair; but until I located Sands, I could not afford to cross him completely off the list.

I paid for my coffee and walked through the cold, lengthening shadows to State Street. I found the City Hall, a white clapboard building which had been freshly painted and had a set of wide wooden schoolhouse steps leading up to the double entrance doors. Inside, there was a short hallway with low counters on both sides. Behind the one on the left were a couple of desks and a large switchboard and two young guys in uniform listening to police calls; the counter on the right belonged to the City Water Department and had a sign midway along reading *Pay Here*. At the end of the hallway was a closed redwood door with *Mayor's Office* etched on it in gold leaf.

One of the uniformed cops—the owner of a blond crewcut and an officious manner—came over to the counter and asked if he could help me. I spread my wallet open so that he could read my identification, and he looked at it as if he could not quite believe what he saw. He read it again, looked at me, read it a third time. "Well," he said, "a private detective," with no inflection at all.

"No kidding," the other cop said. He wore his black hair parted in the middle, like the kid in the old *Our Gang* comedies. He came over and read the identification, and then the two of them stood there staring at me. I thought: Oh Christ, we're not going to play one of those serio-comic sketches now, are we? I had dealt with small-town law enforcement a couple of times before, and they were a breed unto their own: you never quite knew how things were going to go.

But it was all right this time. The blond cop said finally, "Well, hell, you kind of took us by surprise. The closest we get to private eyes up here is on the television."

"Sure, I understand."

"What can we do for you?"

I told him why I was in Roxbury, leaving out some of the non-relevant details. They were willing and talkative, but there was not much either of them could tell me. There had been no incidents of any kind involving a transient just prior to Christmas, and neither had ever heard of a man named Roy Sands. There were no trains that stopped in or about Roxbury, passenger or freight. There were no taxis operating in the village, and no one had sanction to hire out a private vehicle for the transportation of passengers. Hitchhiking was of course illegal, and the law was strictly enforced, especially within the city limits. There were no automobile-rental agencies or dealerships; you had to go to Eureka or Redding or Weaverville.

I had no other angles to ask them about; we had covered the spectrum of immediate possibilities. I thanked them for their time, asked them to make a note of Sands' name and to contact me in San Francisco if anything developed that might shed some light on his disappearance; I gave the blond guy one of my business cards. Then we said good night and I left City Hall and wandered back to Main Street.

Now what? I asked myself. Canvass the town—cafés, bars, cigar stores, and the like? That seemed the only thing to do, eighty percent of investigative accomplishment being legwork; any cop, past or present, could tell you that. So I wasted an hour and a half patrolling both sides of Main, a little of State, a little of Portland Street on the opposite side. Fat zero.

It was after seven now, full dark, and I was hungry. There was a chuck-wagon grill near where I had parked my car, and I went in there and pondered over a rib steak and a cold draft beer. The nagging prescience was still with me, and it was an irritating, frustrating thing because there was no reason for it, no way to explain it or dispel it. Was there something I had overlooked somewhere along the line? Was there something I had failed to consider? More rhetorical questions for which I had no immediate answers.

Another beer and a couple of cigarettes, and it was eight-thirty. I was very tired from too much driving, too much walking, too much thinking. I decided I would return to the Redwood Lodge and get some sleep; I did not want to have to drive back to San Francisco just yet—but in order to justify my remaining here, I had to have something to work on, a direction. Maybe a decent night's rest and the cold light of morning would open up some potentiality of which I was unable to think tonight.

I took the car back to the motel. They had floodlights set up along the side of the road, illuminating the jungle of ferns fronting the office with soft yellow light; a large red-wood sign above the office entrance told you the name of the place and that there was *Vacancy*. I drove past there, and along the graveled half-moon to where number five sat darkly among the gray-black shapes of the trees.

A chill wind blew through the densely grown vegetation, ruffling leaves, bending branches, making soft and lament-ing sounds in the night. It was very dark back there, and I had the vague thought that they ought to have put some kind of floodlighting on the cabins, too, to circumvent ac-cidents and customer complaints. I took the key out of my pocket and started up onto the small porch in front.

And he came out of the ebon shadows on the right, a huge man-form with one arm drawn back, footfalls sliding harshly on the foliated gravel, and hit me across the side of the head with a fist like a stone pestle.

Seventeen

Bright white light fragmented behind my eyes, and I staggered backward, going down on my left side. I thought: *Jesus—who?* and tried to roll over, but he was there and swinging and the pestle slammed into me again, high on the cheekbone. I felt blood flowing warm down the side of my face.

He straddled me, spewing hot sour breath and flecks of spittle, beating at my face, scraping my scalp into the gravel again and again, bringing hot flaring pain and rage, wild rage, you son of a bitch, you son of a bitch, and I levered up at him with my hips, twisting, rolling, pulling free. I got up on my knees and he had his balance back and he hit me again, oh *goddamn* it, and there was more swimming pain, I could barely see him through a red haze of blood and fury.

I crawled away like a crab, gasping, spitting blood, choking on blood, and stumbled up, and he was rushing me, then, low in a crouch with his arms curled wide like a frigging Hollywood ape. I knew who it was in that moment, recognized the rubber mask even more grotesque and unreal now —it was Holly, Holly, and I tried to turn away but it was too late, he slammed into me and we went down, rolling, one of his hands trying to crush my genitals and the other clubbing at my face.

The night was alive in humming, buzzing, pounding noise, but it was all inside my head. I lifted an elbow in reflex

151

and hit him in the face with it, heard him grunt, felt him stiffen, and hit him again, the bastard, hit him again, broke his nose, and the blood spurted down on me like warm, foul rain and I kept on hitting him, pitching him backward, pitching him off of me. He rolled to one side and shook his head bull-like, wanting to get up, and I went after him with the fury still flaming inside me, clasping both hands together and swinging them at his head like a baseball bat. But it was a glancing blow and he kicked at my ankle, falling away, and I was down flat again with him crying and grunting, scrabbling toward me.

I tried to gain my feet, but I had very little strength left, I was hurt all right, I was confused and the fear was there to feed the rage, and that wild anger was all I had left—that and self-preservation and some instinctive things you never forget if you've ever been trained by the military. He slashed at me again, turning my face into the gravel, and more pain flared and I tasted my own blood, hot and thick and salt-sweet. I was half crazy with all of it.

I kicked at him blindly, missed, kicked again, felt the side of my shoe scrape along his rib cage. He shouted in agony, maybe I broke some of his ribs, and then his weight was gone and I was able to roll over and come up. I saw him and threw myself at the dark panting shape and hit him in the same ribs again with my shoulder while he was trying to recover. He screamed a second time, twisting his body, and I went after him on my knees, flailing at him with wild, ineffectual blows at first, until I got to him, and then connecting, hitting him now, hurting him now.

I stopped swinging at him after a time, and he knelt there on all fours with his head hanging down, bull-like again, a fighting bull after the picadors and banderilleros and matadores have finished wounding him and sapping his strength and preparing him for the kill. I raised over him, matador readying the final thrust with the muleta, this crazily disjointed thought there in my mind amid the agony

152

and the heat, and I caught my hands together again and brought them down on the back of Holly's neck. He grunted, not falling, and I brought the hands down again, and again, beating him to the ground, beating him flat, kept on hitting him until I could not raise my arms any longer and he was lying there very still. All of it drained out of me at once, and I thought: I killed him—but I had no reaction to that. I fell away from him, stretching out on my belly on the hard, rough gravel, leaking blood, trying to breathe, trying to regain control.

A long time passed, and no one came, and I thought: We made enough noise to raise half the town, why isn't someone here? But even as I thought that, I knew it wasn't true; the accelerated speed at which things had happened, the heightening of all my senses, the pain and the fury, had magnified things out of proportion. We had not made as much noise as all that, the office was too far away, the fight had not lasted nearly as long as it seemed. We were alone back there in the darkness.

I felt my thoughts clearing finally, in spite of a raging inferno of agony in my head, and I got my weak arms under me and pushed myself up, struggling to a sitting position. I was still gasping. I looked over at Holly, and he had not moved. Droplets of blood fell from somewhere on my face to spatter on the gravel between my knees as I sat there. Get up, I thought. I made it onto my feet, shakily, and stood there hurting until I was sure I could walk all right without falling down. Then I went to Holly and leaned over him, and I could hear the stertorous wheezing of his breath into the gravel. I got a grip on the collar of his torn poplin jacket and dragged him to the cabin porch.

It took some doing to get him up the five steps and across the porch and into the cabin, but I managed it. I left him lying on the floor just inside, and closed the door and locked it and put the key in my pocket. I walked across to the bathroom and flicked on the light, leaving the door open so I could watch him out there, and looked at myself in the mirror over the sink.

Sweet Christ!

I caught onto the sides of the basin with shaking hands, fighting down nausea. I was drenched in blood. The left side of my face was like raw ground beef, pebbled with bits of gravel, dirt commingled with the fluid there. A three-cornered flap of loose skin hung open high on my right cheek, and the eye above it was swollen half shut; bruises on both temples, my upper lip split in two places. There was pain all across the back of my skull where he had rolled it in the gravel, and inside my head a near-unbearable pressure had gathered, like volatile gases coming to an explosion point.

He had done a job on me, all right.

I stripped off my shirt and jacket and ran warm water into the basin, glancing into the other room with my good eye from time to time; Holly had not moved. I washed my face, gently, trying not to cry out. I used a soft towel, and looked in the mirror again, and it was not quite so bad now; but I had to do something about that flap of skin hanging loose under my eye. It was still bleeding, trailing crimson down my cheek in a hellish tear stream.

I went into the other room, moving on enervated legs, and unlocked the front door and stumbled down to my car. There was a first-aid kit in the glove compartment, and I took that back inside, relocking the door. I poured Mercurochrome onto a gauze square and tore off two strips of adhesive tape and stuck them across the top of the pad; then I set my teeth and shut my eyes and placed the bandage gently over the cut, pressing the loose skin back into place.

I could feel the pain down through my groin, and a kind of whimper came out of my throat. After a moment the pain went away and I could breathe again. I poured more Mercurochrome onto some cotton swabbing and worked that over the left side of my face, and then I sat down on the edge of the bed and ate four aspirin dry from the kit.

In my open suitcase I located a package of cigarettes. I tore it open and lit one, drawing in the smoke, coughing, inhaling again. My hands were still trembling; I had not been in a slugging fight in ten years, and never one like this. I was too goddamn old for anything as physical as this, and the reaction was setting in. I thought: He's like a bull, all right, just like a bull. How the hell did I take him?

I sat on the bed and smoked and trembled, and finally I began to feel a little better. The throbbing gentled in my head, and some of the terrible weakness in my legs and arms went away. I walked into the bathroom again and drank a glass of water and came out and looked down at Holly. He was stirring now, moaning deep in his throat.

He rolled over onto his back, and I saw that he looked as bad as I did—blood all over him, cuts, torn clothing, his nose twisted to one side and still flowing, a tooth missing in the front. I backed off a couple of steps, thinking: I hope he doesn't try to start it up again, I don't think I can handle any more. There was a writing desk in one corner of the room, and I went there and took the heavy redwood chair and stood it between Holly and me. If he made another play, I was going to use the chair on him and the hell with it.

Holly lay with his eyes shut, his belly heaving like a giant bellows as he sucked in breath through his broken nose and ruined mouth. Then he moaned and rolled over again and crawled up onto all fours; he shook his head, shook it again, prying his eyes open. He raised one hand, rubbed the back of it across his face, and then he saw me and my hands tensed on the back of the chair.

But he just knelt there, looking at me with his vacuous eyes. After an interval he let the lower half of his body relax, rolling his left hip onto the floor and resting his weight on that and on his left arm. He forced words through his thick lips, "You beat me. Nobody ever beat me before, and you beat me."

"You son of a bitch."

155

"You're tough," Holly said. "You're a tough guy."

"Yeah," I said. "Oh yeah, I'm a tough guy."

"Nobody ever beat me before."

There was a certain respect in his voice, as if he held no more anger or animosity toward me, as if I was now a kind of hero for having beaten him. The bloody mask of his face was expressionless, but I had that feeling of grudging worship and it made me uneasy. I wanted to hate him, and yet I could not do it with him the way he was—a sort of huge child, a worshiping Brahma child. I stood there, trembling, watching him.

"I waited for you two hours," he said. "You didn't come."

"How did you know where to find me?"

"Roxbury ain't big."

"Yeah."

"I know Mr. Jardine. He said you was in number five."

"All right, now the big question: why?"

"Huh?"

"Why did you jump me?"

"You upset Mrs. Emery today."

"Oh, that's some fine reason."

"You're a friend of his, that other one."

"What other one? You mean Sands?"

"Yeah, him."

"I'm not a friend of his, I'm just trying to find him."

"That ain't what you told Mrs. Emery."

"Did she send you after me?"

"She don't know nothing about it."

"It was all your idea, huh?"

"Yeah."

"Just because of Sands."

"He killed Miss Diane. And you're his friend."

"Christ!"

"You deserved same as he got," Holly said.

I stared at him. A vague chill touched my back, staying

on there in the saddle of it. "What?" I said. "What did you say?"

He pressed his thick bluish lips together.

"Did you jump Sands the same way you did me, Holly?"

Silence.

"Goddamn it, Holly, did you?"

"Yeah," he muttered.

"Why?"

"I told you. He caused Miss Diane to die. I heard him tell Mr. and Mrs. Emery what he done, and Mrs. Emery she started screaming for him to leave and Mr. Emery was all excited and took to drinking like he does, and when that guy left I just went after him. I had to do something. The Emerys, they're just like my folks, they been real good to me. Miss Diane was real good to me, too, before she went away. I couldn't just let that guy walk away without doing nothing."

"Where did you jump him? Here at the motel?"

"No."

"Well, where?"

"I followed him in the truck. I offered him a ride."

"You took him somewhere?"

"Yeah."

"Where?"

"To Hammock Grove."

"What's that?"

"A picnic place out at the end of Coachman Road."

"And then what?"

"I hit him a few times."

"You beat him up."

"Yeah. He wasn't tough at all."

"What did you do then?"

"I left him there. I drove away."

"Was he alive?"

He stared up at me. "I never killed nobody."

"You're sure he was alive?"

157

"I told you, didn't I?"

"Was he unconscious?"

"I guess so."

"Where did you leave him?"

"In Hammock Grove."

"*Where* in Hammock Grove?"

"By the bridge."

"What bridge?"

"There's this bridge goes across a little creek," Holly said. "When you first come in to the picnic area."

"All right. What time of day did all this happen?"

"In the afternoon."

"What time?"

"I dunno. It was still light out."

"And afterward you went home, back to the Emery farm?"

"Yeah."

"Do the Emerys know what you did?"

"No, I never told nobody."

"And you never saw Sands again?"

"No," Holly said. "Can I get up now? My head hurts."

I kept my hands on the chair back. "Get up, then."

It took him several seconds. He stood, finally, swaying a little, as if he were very dizzy. He said, "You hurt me plenty."

I did not answer.

He moved then, away from me, into the bathroom. I watched him running water into the basin, as I had done, washing the blood from his face. He did not look into the mirror. He picked up the same towel I had used and buried his face in it, and then threw it down again and came out into the main room, blinking at me.

"What you going to do?" he said. "You going to take me to the police?"

I just stared at him.

"I don't like to be locked up. I can't stand that."

"You can't go around jumping people like you've been doing."

"I won't do it no more."

"How do I know you won't?"

"Well, I won't."

"All right," I said, "get out of here." I was near exhaustion now, and even if I wanted to take him in I did not think I was capable of it. I would pass out before we got half-way to the City Hall, with him docile or not. "Go on, Holly, go home."

"You won't come bothering Mrs. Emery no more, will you?"

"No," I said, "I won't come around there any more."

"I got nothing against you now," Holly said. "You beat me, and nobody ever done that before. You're a tough guy."

He staggered over to the door and got it open and looked at me with that pathetic, battered rubber mask; then he went out into the night, pulling the door shut behind him.

I moved directly to the light switch and put the room in darkness. I sat on the bed and took the rest of my clothes off and lay back with the blanket over me, trying to think; but it was no good, it was just no good.

I let sleep wash over me, wrapping the throbbing pain in it. Tomorrow I could think, tomorrow . . .

Eighteen

I awoke to a consummate aching stiffness of every muscle in my body.

It was after nine and there was sunlight in the room, shining dustily in long, pale shafts on the bare redwood floor. I lay for a time with my eyes closed against the light, very still, listening to the hammering of surf within the confines of my skull. It began to ebb, finally, and I allowed the blankness upon which I had been concentrating to be filled by returning thoughts of last night.

It seemed like a particularly vivid dream instead of a fragment of reality, the way the events surrounding the knife episode a few months ago had later seemed. I tried to hate Holly again, but that was as useless as it had been last night; he lived in a kind of primitive, simplistic world where everything was black or white, without shading, and if the sanctity of the cave and its dwellers was threatened in any way, you fought as savagely as you knew how to protect those who protected you. There was no way to hate someone like that. Maybe, in some ways, his world was just a little better than ours; it was certainly less grim.

I went over the conversation I had had with Holly, examining again what he had told me. It was the truth, of that I was fairly certain. I did not think he would have known how to lie about something like that. He had then, as he'd said, picked up Roy Sands following the visit to the Emery farm on the twentieth of last month; then he had driven him out to this Hammock Grove and leaned on him and left him there unconscious. I was willing to accept that without disputation.

But then what?

Holly had sworn that Sands was alive when he'd left, and I believed that, too. Sands had come back here to the Redwood Lodge later to pick up his belongings, hadn't he? And yet, if he was hurt, why hadn't he gone to the police to press charges against Holly? Or to a doctor—who in turn would have notified the authorities because of the nature of those injuries? If he had done either, the cops would have had his name on record. So what *had* Sands done after coming out of it? Well—had he come out of it at all? Holly had just left him there, unconscious, and maybe he had been hurt worse than Holly thought, had had a concussion or some such, remained comatose, perhaps died of exposure . . . ? No, if that were the case, the body would have been found by this time—unless Hammock Grove was the kind of summer picnic area no one ever went to in the winter, and it had been less than a month since December 20—oh Christ, if he had died out there, how could he have picked up his stuff and gone up to Eugene? I was thinking in pointless circles.

I swung my feet out of bed and got up gingerly and took a couple of experimental steps that seemed to work out all right. In the bathroom I tried the mirror again and it was not as bad as I expected; the swelling was gone from the one eye, and the left side of my face, under the red-orange streaks of the Mercurochrome, had begun to scab already. The cut on my cheekbone ached painfully, and I thought about taking the bandage off to apply some more antiseptic; but that did not seem like such a good idea, remembering that flap of skin, and I decided I would be wiser to leave it alone.

I knew I was going to have to see a doctor sometime today, to have the cut and the other abrasions looked at, and

I did not relish the thought. Still, it had to be done and I accepted that. I did not see any point in making a report to the local cops; if I did that, I would have to give them Holly's name—and no purpose would be served in having the poor bastard jailed. He was all right as long as no one bothered the Emerys, and who was going to bother them now?

I used a little more of the Mercurochrome on my upper lip and the side of my face, and on my scalp, and combed my hair, and ran the toothbrush around inside my mouth a couple of times; there was no sense in trying to shave or wash. I wondered what Cheryl would say when she saw me, and then I knew she would take it all right after the initial shock; she was not like Erika. I would have had to put up with a lecture from Erika, but there would be no lecture from Cheryl. The difference between the two of them was like night and day.

There was one of those instant-coffee dispensers in the room, and I made myself a cup and drank it, sitting on the desk chair. I had no desire to frighten hell out of some waitress in a local café coming in the way I looked, and I was not in any mood for breakfast anyway. The thing that had been nagging at me while I had eaten supper the previous evening was back and stronger than ever, nurtured by the revelation that Holly had jumped on Roy Sands the way he had on me. It was all starting to come together, I could sense that: the answer was here in Roxbury, and it was very close.

I finished my coffee and gathered up the bloodstained clothing. Then I soaked the towel both Holly and I had used in cold water and got down stiffly and washed the dried blood from the floor where he had lain, where both of us had spattered fluid walking back and forth. When I straightened again, I was breathing asthmatically and my arms and legs felt weak. I wadded everything together and took it out into the fresh clean morning air and dumped it into the trunk of my car.

I slid under the wheel, then, and swung around to the

163

right of the office. There was a dark green Pontiac pulled up in front of number seven; Jardine had finally gotten another customer. Well, maybe things were starting to look up for everybody now.

I drove out to Coachman Road and onto it, passing the Emery farm and seeing no one out and around. I wanted to have a look at Hammock Grove before I saw a doctor; there might be nothing to learn out there, but I was still fresh out of other possibilities.

A couple of miles further along Coachman Road, the firs and redwoods seemed to grow thicker and there was less sunlight filtering through the ceiling of leaves and branches overhead. I had the window down, and the smell of the woods filled the car with a kind of spicy redolence that was a narcotic for the pulsing ache in my head.

Around a sharp bend I came upon a very narrow paved road leading off to the left, and a wooden sign at the junction, reading: HAMMOCK GROVE, and below that: PICNICKING · CAMPING · HIKING. I turned along there, and it was like following a tunnel through the imposing giant trees; it made you feel very small, very vulnerable, passing at the feet of some of nature's most beautiful creations.

I traveled a quarter of a mile, and then I could see the picnic area spread out in a grotto of sorts, with parking spaces and small stone barbecues and heavy redwood picnic tables and benches. There was a thick double-link chain stretched across the road between two posts at the entrance to the grounds. Beyond that the road twisted and turned and looped back on itself throughout; like the picnic areas and facilities, it was covered with leaves and pine needles and loose topsoil, a result of the heavy winter rains. When spring came, there would be a forestry crew in to clean and rake it out for the influx of weekend Thoreaus and all their screaming multitudes.

I parked nose-up to the chain and got out and stepped

over it, letting my eyes make a slow ambit of the area. The bridge Holly had mentioned was on the left, an arched, log-railed affair that spanned a wide, rocky creek; there was a quick stream within its banks now, although I suspected that it would be completely dry during the summer. It hugged the base of a steep, rounded slope grown with wood ferns and spindly firs that formed the left-hand boundary for the grove; deeper in, it hooked around to run beneath a couple of other wooden bridges through the general middle of the grotto—and behind me, it made the curve with the slope to disappear well back among the redwoods.

Except for the raucous cry of a jay somewhere high in one of the trees, it was very quiet. Cool and damp, too, with very little wind. I walked over toward the bridge and looked into the creek, and there was nothing for me to see except rocks and leaves and cold rushing water. There was nothing in the immediate vicinity of the bridge, either; the wind-swept foliage had long since taken care of any traces.

I scuffed through the leaves near the bridge, for no particular reason, but nothing of interest lay beneath the soft, wet covering. I saw that one of the foot trails which cross-hatched the grounds led to a large brown building with green-latticed entrances on either side: the rest rooms. I walked over, thinking that if I had been Sands and I had woken up from a beating in a place such as this one, I would have made for these rest rooms first thing—looking for water, towels, a mirror to check the damage.

There was a brand-new padlock, undisturbed, on the door marked MEN, and none of the frosted windows had been broken or tampered with. I made a turn of the building and looked in at the side designated WOMEN; nothing there, either, except that the padlock was a little rustier. Well, Sands had not made for the rest rooms then, because even if he had found them locked, he could have broken a window to get inside or shouldered one of the doors open without too much trouble.

What *had* he done, then?

The most logical answer was that he had staggered off down that same road up which I had just driven, and either walked or gotten a ride back to the Redwood Lodge. And if that were the case, I was only wasting my time out here.

I went back and stood at the foot of the bridge. That intuitive sense was working again, and it kept insisting that there was something here for me, something important, and that all I had to do was keep looking in order to find out what it was. I glanced off to my left, and there was an extension of the path coming from the rest rooms; it curved over to run concurrent with the road for some little way. Behind me were two picnic tables set on either side of one of the stone barbecues, and across the bridge in front of me was the slope. The base of it, at the bank of the creek, was fairly level, and contained a path that paralleled the stream in both directions.

The back of my neck felt cold, and I put my right hand up to touch my damaged face. The fingers became immobile. My damaged face, oh Christ, my damaged face! Something dark nudged my mind, and the coldness increased, *damaged face*, and I was moving up and across the bridge before I even considered it. I looked to the right, deeper into the open grove; then I went off to the left, walking slowly, alternating my gaze with the side of the slope and the creek, not seeing anything, moving on instinct.

The path led me well around the slope and then, gradually, away from it, still paralleling the meandering stream. I stopped and glanced back, and I could not see the picnic grotto or the road or my car from where I was; the trees grew thickly here, and the ground was completely carpeted with wet, aromatic leaves.

I started walking again. Up ahead, beside the stream, was a huge fire-gutted redwood stump. I stopped once more, looking at it, and my eyes shifted then to a cluster of large, porous rocks at the low creek bank just beyond the stump.

There were several of them, bunched closely together, and I stared at them and kept staring at them. Something wrong there, something wrong . . .

And I had it: the biggest of the rocks, maybe three feet in circumference, was bleached gray along the top and stained a much darker color along its bottom surface, as if that part of the rock had lain in the acid soil for a long time before being recently uprooted and partially revolved.

I went over and stood by the cluster, and there was a kind of leaden nausea in the pit of my stomach. I knew what I was going to find, had known from the moment there by the bridge. It took me a scant two minutes to shoulder the rocks out of the way, to uncover the shallow grave which had been dug beneath them—and the ugly, decomposing thing which lay within it.

Roy Sands was no longer among the missing.

Nineteen

The side of his head had been crushed by a blow from some heavy, blunt instrument—very probably the stained and rusted tire iron which lay alongside the body. The condition of his clothes, his flesh, the nesting presence of insects— God!—told me that he had been in there for some time, and even though there was not much left of the face for positive identification, I had no doubt at all that it was Sands.

The nausea came boiling up into my throat, and I turned away and walked stiffly to the blackened redwood stump. I leaned against that and dragged air into my lungs, and momentarily the feeling passed. A couple of blackbirds chattered in a slender thread of sunlight nearby, and then flew off together; it was very still again.

The whole sick business began to take shape in my mind. I knew beyond a doubt now the nature of the thing that had been nagging at me, the thing I had failed to consider because there had been no reason for considering it, the thing that had been subconsciously bothering me all along with its lack of rhyme or reason, its alien presence in the pattern of events as I had uncovered them.

I had been able to find no reason why Sands would have gone to Eugene, Oregon, and that was because *he had never gone there.* He had not sent those wires, had not been the man who checked into the transient hotel, he was dead then, he was dead and buried under those rocks behind me. The entire thing with Eugene had been a red herring, a fact I had finally guessed when I touched my face there by the bridge. Sands had been beaten by Holly, and it was incontrovertible that such a beating would have left his face as swollen and discolored and marked as mine; but neither the hotel nor the Western Union clerk had mentioned Sands as having looked battered and broken—a fact they could not have helped but notice despite a hat and a muffler and a coat with a turned-up collar, a fact one or both would have related to me.

So it was not Sands they saw, it was his murderer, the guy who had come in here after Holly left.

It had to be that way. You could figure it, and it was simple now: the guy had done the killing and buried the body, after first taking Sands' motel key off the corpse, his wallet, and any other identification which might have been there. Then he had returned to the Redwood Lodge, slipped into Sands' unit, and packed everything in the single suitcase. In his own car he had driven up to Eugene, and on Tuesday night, the twenty-first, he had sent those wires and he had registered at the Leavitt Hotel. Later that evening, or the next morning, he had simply walked out, leaving the suitcase there with Sands' stuff in it.

End of the line.

In the beginning he had *wanted* an investigation, because that investigation would begin with the Eugene angle —the wires to California—and would eventually turn up the hotel angle, the packed suitcase, would eventually conclude with the logical assumption that the baffling disappearance had happened in Oregon. That was why no wire had been sent to Elaine Kavanaugh—to deepen the mystery. And he had figured, rightly, that a hat and a muffler and a turned-up collar would be an effective disguise—no one else but Holly knew about the beating—and that an investigator would have no reason to doubt that the man had been Sands, that a scrawled signature in a hotel register was authentic.

But my particular investigation had not stopped at the

170

dead end in Oregon. Elaine Kavanaugh had insisted that I go to Germany, and this was something the killer had not bargained for. He had not wanted me snooping around over there, uncovering the connection between Sands and Diane Emery, and so in panic he had made those threatening telephone calls to Elaine and me in the wild hope that they would prevent excavations at Kitzingen. All they had succeeded in doing, of course, was assuring me that there *was* something to be learned in Germany—but panic and fear are usually irrational, especially when murder is their catalyst.

So it had to be someone Sands knew and knew well; someone who had been aware of the debts incurred in the poker game, the amount of those debts, in order to send the wires from Eugene; someone who had hated Roy Sands for an as yet undetermined reason, and who had known he was coming to Roxbury, and who had followed him, and who had waited his chance and then moved in and killed him. It had to be the same man who had stolen the portrait from my apartment, who had made the calls. Nick Jackson was out of it now; he could not have known about those poker debts, or that Sands was coming to Roxbury—much less about the portrait of Sands and that Elaine Kavanaugh had given it to me, or about my trip to Germany in the few hours elapsed between the decision and the threatening calls. No, it had to be one of Sands' three service buddies, the way it had seemed all along—Hendryx or Rosmond or Gilmartin.

Which one?

Which *one?*

The portrait—why was the portrait important, why had it been stolen? To prevent me from showing it in Eugene, because in its clear, sharp detailing it was better than any photograph and might perhaps destroy the careful masquerade the killer had undertaken there? Yeah, that was certain to be part of the reason; but I had the feeling that there was more to it than that, something deeper and, if less rational, even more important to the man who had murdered Roy

171

Sands. A pattern was beginning to take shape now, and it was an ugly pattern, one of jealousy and love and hate, one of twisted human emotions that had culminated in cold-blooded murder . . .

I stood with all of these answers and half-answers spinning free-fall inside my head, with the thing that had been Roy Sands lying crushed and huddled in the shallow grave a few feet behind me. I turned away, stumbling a little, and started back along the path toward the bridge and my car. The one thing I knew I had to do immediately was to contact the authorities.

My shoe scuffling through the profusion of leaves was the only sound—and then there was another, suddenly, an unmistakable metallic sound.

I stopped abruptly to listen. Nothing now, no blackbirds, no jays, just the teasing wind. My heart began to slug faster, and I went forward again, coming to the junction of slope and path and creek, moving past it, around the slope to where I could see the picnic grove and my car—my car with the hood raised and somebody, a man, I could not see his face, jerking at something inside there.

I began to run.

I ran along the path without thinking, acting on reflex, opening my mouth to shout, and strangling the cry; needles of pain lanced through my body from the exertion of aching muscles. I reached the bridge and started over it, too late remembering how noise carries in a quiet forest area; the slap of my shoes on the wooden planking was like the hollow cracking of whips. He looked up, the briefest of glances in my direction, and I still could not see his face, he had a plaid hunter's jacket on and a hunter's cap pulled down and he had a rifle held loosely by the stock; I felt the instinctive urge to throw myself flat and gain some kind of cover, faltering, running toward the center of the picnic grotto in a diagonal trajectory because cover was there.

The guy turned and fled.

Dark trousers and the jacket flapping loose above, the rifle extended out on his right and him running spindle-legged down the road. My lungs were on fire, but I managed to change direction, going after him, seeing him disappear around the bend in the road, vaulting the double-link chain, stumbling past my car, almost falling, mouth open and sucking air like a blowfish, thinking: Let him go, he'll kill you, he killed Sands, you're no goddamn hero. But I kept on running; it was as if I could not bring myself up, as if I was running on a belt with no way to stop.

A sudden roaring dissolved the stillness of the woods, an automobile engine coming to life; he had wheels parked somewhere along the road. I staggered around the bend, and a hundred yards ahead a car was pulling away, tires howling, spraying soft dirt—a green car, a green Pontiac, the same green Pontiac I had seen in front of number seven at the Redwood Lodge a little earlier that same morning.

I stopped running, gasping, watching the car hurtle down the road. He followed me up here, I thought, he followed me from San Francisco, followed me out to Hammock Grove this morning—and I turned, running again back to my car.

Lungs screaming, I leaned over the fender, looking into the engine compartment. He had pulled all of the spark-plug wires loose, and the rotor was missing. If he had taken that goddamn rotor with him . . .

I made a soft, meaningless sound in my throat, and rubbed thick sweat out of my eyes, and tried to get my breathing down to normal. Goddamn cigarettes, the goddamn weeds, oh, the goddamn filthy goddamn coffin nails! directing rage and impotent frustration at the handiest outlet. I pressed my cheek against the cold metal surface of the fender, and after a hellish long time my lungs cleared and I could function.

I went looking for the rotor, maybe he had thrown it away, he *had* to have thrown it away. Another five minutes went by, a year went by, and there it was, lying on a bed of leaves thirty feet from the car. I took it back and got it into place, and then went to work on the plug wires. It took time, time, and I could not seem to locate the proper sequence; the car was old and the firing order had not been stamped on the engine block, as with the newer models. I discovered once that I was shouting obscenities, and closed my mouth to cut that off, and the sweat ran in rivers along my body. My lungs ached and my body ached. I wanted to lie down somewhere in the cool shade of one of the redwoods, to sleep, to rest. But I kept at it, and finally I knew I had the right progression; when I kicked the engine over this time, it caught and held.

I got the hood down and backed the car around and headed back to Roxbury. I drove too fast, hunched over the wheel, trying not to think, to concentrate only on the driving. But I was thinking just enough, just enough.

Why hadn't he killed me back there, with that rifle? Why hadn't he shot me when he had the chance, why had he just disabled the car and not very effectively at that? One answer, one possibility, and I felt physically sick because it was too late now, I knew in my mind that it was too late now.

I came into Roxbury and off on the left was the Redwood Lodge. The green Pontiac was there, in front of number seven, slewed up to the front porch. *Too late, too damned late.* My foot came jamming down on the brakes, and I heard them lock with a screaming of metal and the tires screaming in a different cadence on the macadam, the machine yawing this way and that. I fought the wheel, wrenching it hard to the left—more screaming—and then I was onto the graveled half-moon and braking next to the Pontiac, jumping out with the engine still throbbing, swaying up onto the porch. The door was standing partially ajar, oh Jesus, and I put the flat of my hand against the wood and shoved it wide.

He was there.

He was turning, very slowly, in the center of the room, suspended from one of the rafter beams by a length of hemp rope looped around his neck, his head lolling to one side, neck broken, eyes staring, turning, dead.

Doug Rosmond had hanged himself, just as Diane Emery had done in Kitzingen, Germany, less than three months before.

Twenty

The only thing I could think was: What am I going to say to Cheryl, what am I going to *say?*

I stood motionless in the doorway, staring at Rosmond, watching him turn at the end of that taut rope, hearing the rope creak slightly, nightmarishly, from his weight. I stood there for long, frozen seconds, asking myself again and again in a kind of frightening singsong, like the words of a monstrous jingle running through my mind: What am I going to say to Cheryl, what am I going to say? Then, finally, I was able to move and I stepped inside and shut the door behind me and leaned against it, still staring at Rosmond, and his face dissolved like something in quicklime and became Cheryl's face and I was filled with an ugly, suffocating, poisonous bile.

I took another step forward, and I could not look at him any longer. I turned away and there was a mirror on the wall over the room's writing desk. I could see myself clearly reflected in the glass. I had an insane urge to smash the mirror, the hideous, twisted, red-orange-black-pink face that stared back at me. I fought it down, turning again, and Rosmond filled the room, his body and that goddamn gallows creaking, creaking, as he turned there on the stretched rope. The bile churned in my belly and I started to back up, wanting air; for the first time, then, I saw on the varnished top of the writing desk some sheets of paper folded in half—

motel stationery—and something written in heavy pencil on the back of the facing sheet.

It was my name.

I put my hand out and touched the papers and then took it away again. I did not want to read what was there, I wanted to read what was there, I did not want to know, I had to know. I swept the papers up and got to the door, pulling it open—and Jardine was out there with a couple of other people. They stared at me, backing off a few steps when they saw my face, and Jardine said, "My God, what happened to you? What are you doing in there, that's not your—"

"Shut up," I said.

"Listen—"

"There's a dead man in there, call the police."

Somebody gasped, and Jardine looked pale and faint. "What? A dead man? Oh God, you—"

"Call the police," I said. "Call the police."

He retreated and the others went with him, staring at me. Then they began to run in a pack toward the lodge office. I sank down onto the porch steps and my eyes were on the crumpled sheets of paper in my hand. I stared at them for a long moment, and then I opened them and read the hurried pencil-scrawled lines covering the white inner surfaces:

Its been coming to this for a long time & when I saw you out there this morning going toward his grave I knew this was the only way out. I couldnt shoot you even though thats what I thought I would do, I couldnt do it. I had you in the sights walking over there on the slope but I couldnt pull the trigger, I kept thinking of Cheryl & what you mean to her, how shes come alive these past few days. She was dead til she met you, she didnt care about anything, then you came, I couldnt shoot you. I love my sister & if I killed you I would be killing her too

178

you see. Its better me because of what I did. I dont know if you found his grave or not but it doesnt matter now, its there under a cluster of rocks by a gutted stump. I killed him, you would have found out it was me, I was staying here at this motel when he died. Cheryl told me you were back from Germany & going away again today & didnt want me to know so it had to be youd found out about Diane & Roxbury & this was where you were going. She didnt want to tell me because of her promise but I dragged it out of her, I knew she saw you it was in her eyes yesterday morning. She didnt know she could be helping to kill you & thats another reason I couldnt shoot you. Maybe you know already why I killed Sands but maybe not all of it & I better put it down here. I did it because of Diane. He was laying her for months, he kept it a secret because of Elaine but finally he had to tell somebody about it & it was me. He wanted to break it off with her but he couldnt do it, every time he tried she wouldnt listen & got him into bed with her so he wanted me to do it. I said I would, we were buddies, & I went to Diane & tried to get her to break it off but she loved him, she couldnt help it she loved him. It was crazy but then I fell in love with her, I never loved nobody before not that way, I never thought I could. I loved Diane though, I told her I loved her after awhile but she wanted him & I was going crazy with loving her knowing he was with her all the time & not caring anything about her except she was a piece of ass. I began to hate him as much as I loved her, then she got knocked up & wanted him to marry her but he wouldnt do it he had Elaine. She hung herself over him, I almost died when I found out. I had my service 45 & I was going to use it on myself that night but then I thought no, that would be too easy, what about Sands, he had to be punished, it was his fault she was dead. I knew I was going to kill him then but he stayed on Larson & I just had no chance to do it, not until SF & he told

179

me he was going up here to see her parents, he was still feeling guilty over her being dead on account of him. I rented a car like I did to follow you and followed him when he walked out to the Emerys, I was going to kill him when he started back but that hired man picked him up in the truck. I was behind them going out to the grove & I watched the hired man beat Sands up when they got there. I went half crazy seeing it and when the hired man left & Sands was lying there all bloody I drove up & took the tire iron out and killed him with it. I took his body over to those rocks and buried him, then I got the idea to take his stuff to Oregon & send the telegrams to put everybody off the track. I thought I had this perfect murder but theres no such thing. You came along & you had that picture of Roy, Chuck told me about it & I knew Diane had drawn it. I couldnt let you show it around Eugene, maybe that hotel clerk would see it wasnt Roy who checked in that night & I wanted it because Diane had drawn it even if it was of him, I wanted it the minute I heard about it I cant explain it any better than that. I couldnt think of any other way except to break into your place, it was a stupid thing but I had to have it & I knew you were out with Cheryl. Then you said you were going to Germany & I tried to stop you with those calls, I wouldnt have killed you or Elaine then but I thought I could scare you, I didnt want you to find out about Diane & I knew you would because you had the name of that gallery, I knew if you went it would be all over, youd find out somehow about me & Roxbury. I think I knew right when you didnt pay any attention to the warning & went anyway it was going to come to this. I shouldnt have come up here, but I did it & I couldnt kill you & now its over, now I know what I have to do. I cant stand the idea of being locked up in a cage & anyway whats left for me, Diane is dead & I revenged her with Sands & I dont have anything to live for, only Cheryl & now she *has you somebody decent & its better for her this way with me dead & you to take care of her, its better for all of us this way. Take care of her, love her, & Im sorry about Elaine but not sorry about Sands, I cant wait any longer now I have the rope from the hardware store*

Doug Rosmond

I lowered the pages and put my head in my hands. *Take care of her, love her* . . . Oh, God, love and hate and death, why can't it be simple, why can't it be uncomplicated, why can't love triumph and goodness triumph and there be no death and no pain? Two women sitting back there in San Francisco, waiting, waiting, and I have to tell them that the two men closest to them are dead, dead of love, dead of hate, dead of this goddamn frigging unyielding world, and how am I going to tell them, Elaine and Cheryl—Cheryl, *take care of her, love her* . . .

Siren sounds. I raise my head, and a powder-blue police car comes hurtling into the Redwood Lodge, rocks to a stop. Two uniformed cops come out, one of them the blond guy I spoke with the day before, running with drawn guns in their hands. I get to my feet, still clutching the papers, and go to meet them on trembling legs.

What am I going to say to Cheryl?

What am I going to say?

Made in the USA
Monee, IL
04 November 2023

45801709R00109